American Short Fiction

PUBLISHED IN COOPERATION WITH
THE TEXAS CENTER FOR WRITERS
Rolando Hinojosa Smith, Director,

AND WITH THE SOUND OF WRITING,
A SHORT STORY MAGAZINE OF THE AIR,
BROADCAST ON NATIONAL PUBLIC RADIO,
Caroline Marshall, Executive Producer

Volume 1, Number 2, Summer 1991

UNIVERSITY OF TEXAS PRESS

AMERICAN SHORT FICTION, established in 1991, is published four times a year by the University of Texas Press in cooperation with the Texas Center for Writers and "The Sound of Writing," a short story magazine of the air broadcast on National Public Radio. The editor invites submissions of fiction of all lengths from short shorts to novellas. All stories will be selected for publication based on their originality and craftsmanship.

STYLE *The Chicago Manual of Style* is used in matters of form. Manuscripts must be double-spaced throughout.

MANUSCRIPTS AND EDITORIAL CORRESPONDENCE Please send all submissions to: American Short Fiction, Parlin 14, Department of English, University of Texas at Austin, Austin, Texas 78712-1164. Manuscripts are accepted only from September 1 through May 31 of each academic year. Please accompany submissions with a stamped, self-addressed envelope.

SUBSCRIPTIONS (ISSN 1051-4813) Individuals/$24.00; Institutions/$36.00. Foreign subscribers please add $4.00 to each subscription order. Single Copies: Individuals/$7.95; Institutions/$9.00. Send subscriptions to: American Short Fiction, Journals Division, University of Texas Press, Box 7819, Austin, Texas 78713.

Design and typography by George Lenox

COVER: *Mexico Bajo La Lluvia L2,* 1986, 19 x 24⅞ inches
four-color lithograph by Vicente Rojo,
from the portfolio *Mexico Nueve*. In the collection of the
Archer M. Huntington Art Gallery at the University of Texas at Austin.
Gift of the Tamarind Institute, 1988.

ONTENTS

"The Overcoat" by Gina Berriault, "Piano Lessons" by David Michael Kaplan, "A Pool of Fish" by Lewis Nordan, and "Three-Dollar Dogs" by William Kittredge are published courtesy of "The Sound of Writing," a short story magazine of the air broadcast on National Public Radio.

LAURA FURMAN

THE EDITOR'S NOTES

I enjoy particularly the experience of reading a long story. As a reader one makes a commitment to a piece of fiction—just as the writer does—and settling into the long story promises one a relationship of some endurance. Some of my favorite works of literature are uncategorizable, or at least it is possible to name them variously as stories, novellas, short novels: *The Spoils of Poynton* by Henry James, *Pale Horse, Pale Rider* by Katherine Anne Porter, and *The Pilgrim Hawk* by Glenway Wescott. The long story is a favorite with writers, though not always with editors. It is a difficult length for a commercial magazine to accommodate, or even for a literary quarterly that must also give over space to poetry, criticism, and essays.

In founding *American Short Fiction,* we have created a new place for works of such length because our pages are reserved for fiction exclusively. Our second issue is a fair demonstration of our commitment to finding and publishing work of high quality, regardless of length.

William Humphrey has written a rich tale about King Lear in the Hudson Valley. One reads it for its sad, stubborn comedy, wishing that the hero were less of a fool and dreading what marvelous disaster he will next invent. In Judith Rossner's long story, the narrator recalls a turning point in her life when a portrait of her future self gives her the key to her freedom. Both stories revolve around the question of possession—of an apple orchard, an oil painting, the fate of a human being.

I have long admired the work of Gina Berriault. Her very short story, "The Overcoat," is powerful, painful, and written on the bones of her character. In Lynn Freed's story, we see a woman's transformation as she learns to survive by being misunderstood. Naguib Mahfouz, his stories seen rarely in English, tells of a magic "Blessed Night" in which the drunken protagonist loses and gains everything. Tama Janowitz presents a crisp, modern fable of a man who mistakes good fortune for good character.

As readers, we seek involvement and commitment from all fiction, long and short, and I found these qualities as I read and selected the work for our second issue. In it are nine works of fiction about parents and children, dying men and sea lions, sweet childhood hopefulness, bitter adult self-destruction, and hard-earned redemption. I hope that the readers of *American Short Fiction* take as much pleasure in the reading of our second issue as I have in the editing.

JUDIT

116TH STREET JENNY

At the beginning of the seventies my parents and my sister and brother were all stable, married and teaching in universities, so that even if the sixties hadn't provided me with the rhetoric to explain dropping out or smoking dope, I might have felt the need to distinguish myself by doing both. In the middle of my sophomore year at Oberlin, I returned to Manhattan and with four friends moved into an apartment on the Lower East Side that was to be a sort of urban commune, a group disengaged from life's crude competitions and petty quarrels, unmoved by the need to plan for the future or take account of the past. Our arrangement lasted into the following autumn only because each of us was away for much of the time during the warm months.

In the early winter, I asked my parents if I could come home. They consented, on the condition that I return to college, Barnard or Columbia's School of General Studies. They both taught at Columbia (my mother, modern art, my father, twentieth-century European history) so that aside from the schools' other virtues, they would not have to pay tuition. Although I didn't yet know this, my parents had applied for joint grants that would take them to the

Orient during the following academic year. They were concerned about renting to strangers or allowing the apartment to remain vacant and were delighted to find, once I'd moved back in, that I had calmed down, was not interested in sharing my living quarters with friends for more than an occasional night, and was willing to act, at least for a while, as though I valued a college degree.

I had grown up in that apartment, one of those huge Riverside Drive aeries built in the days when most large apartments had some provision for a maid, that is to say, for a person without the space and comfort requirements of the normal human being. There were four good-sized bedrooms off a back hallway, then a tiny one next to the kitchen. Moving back, I suggested to my parents that since I'd been away and we'd all had more privacy, it might be just as well for me to sleep in the tiny room; the large bedroom that was still more or less mine could be a study and a second guest room. Of the rooms that had been my sister's and brother's, one had been furnished to suit the housekeepers they hired periodically then fired because they were inadequate as cooks.

My parents had an extremely strong interest in good food. Women hired in spite of their unfamiliarity with our favorites were given a certain length of time to learn them and were fired if they had not. From an early age I had exhibited a strong affinity for the domestic, a tendency to be in the kitchen while everyone else in the family was off at a desk. As I grew up I had become increasingly helpful in the matter of training new housekeeper-cooks, increasingly capable of making a good meal myself. It had been a puzzle to me when I was young, and remained a source of disgruntlement as I grew up, that my parents, for all their culinary obsessiveness, could not accept the notion of food's drawing me more powerfully than academic subjects did.

That summer, while visiting their friends, the painters

Eleanora and Jason Stonepark at their home outside Florence (They'd become friendly when Eleanora was my mother's student), my parents had found and hired to come home with them a woman named Anna Cherubini. Anna's children were running the family's mom-and-pop style restaurant in Florence, for which Anna had been the chef until her husband died the year before. For reasons having to do with the wife of one of her sons, Anna had begun to feel superfluous. After some deliberation she had consented to come to the States to work for my parents "for a little while," tending the apartment and, of course, preparing her lovely meals.

In the course of learning from Anna how to cook her specialties, which included fresh pasta (still unknown in New York outside of the West Village, East Harlem and a couple of high-priced restaurants), and of helping her to translate the recipes for my parents' other favorites, I not only became a much better cook than I'd been, but also learned to speak a decent Italian. Then, in the spring of 1974, Anna got a call from her family saying she was needed at the restaurant. *Rapido*. She went.

All this is by way of explaining how it came to be that on a weekday night when Eleanora and Jason (Her maiden name was Stein, she'd married the person then named Jason Park, and in those days when the debate over keeping one's "own" name, that is to say, one's father's name, hadn't even begun, they had legally changed their last names to Stonepark) were coming to dinner and both my parents had heavy teaching schedules, I cooked and served the meal. When Jason, learning it was my work, congratulated me in Italian and I answered in kind, he asked, still in Italian, whether I had spent time in Italy.

I liked Jason and did not attempt to impress him with the extent of the rebelliousness that had encouraged my parents to send me to camp instead of taking me on their travels, as they had my sister and brother. I was a change-of-life baby, born to a mother whose two real children had been civilized academics almost from birth. I told Jason I'd gone to camp with my friends.

He nodded. "I can understand that. Do your friends share your interest in Italy?"

I grinned. "Pizza's about it."

I wasn't even certain it was legitimate for *me* to claim an affinity. I had become fluent in Italian because of my interest in food and the amount of time I spent with Anna. The food romance and the big-city romance had yet to marry, taking New Yorkers on the honeymoon, and exotic, or even just plain foreign, foods were not available throughout Manhattan as they would be in another few years. Anna, during her first weeks in New York, had always been looking for ingredients she did not, when they were located, deem satisfactory. My parents had initiated her to Zabar's, and Zabar's was all right for cheese and coffee beans (although she would not acknowledge that the Reggiano bought there was identical to the Parmesan she'd grated in Italy), and she would make do with canned tomatoes when the real ones ("*pommadori nostrani*") went out of season. But it was I who had brought her to the Village and lower Second Avenue for sausages, fresh herbs and bread she judged good enough to eat, not to speak of vegetables like finocchio and broccoli rabe that would remain unknown in non-Italian neighborhood stores until the Koreans took them over. My Italian had come in the learning of the food even as I would become facile with Spanish, which I'd studied in school but never used outside it, when Cuban-Chinese restaurants began to flourish along Broadway. I never learned French because I didn't know anyone who spoke it and the cookbooks were available in English.

Jason asked if I knew that he and Eleanora had a home and vineyard in Gaiole that my parents occasionally visited. When I told him I'd heard about the place, which sounded wonderful, he said, "Perhaps you'll come and visit us sometime and see for yourself." I smiled, dismissing the remark as a pleasantry, but as it turned out, he had something quite specific in mind. The following week I accepted an invitation to Sunday lunch at his home. When I asked my father if he knew why I'd been invited, he shrugged and said that I had impressed Jason. When I pushed him to speculate, he said that one of the things he liked about Jason was that if the other man had something to discuss with me, he'd bring it up directly with me. I might bear in mind that my mother had a very high opinion of Eleanora Stonepark's talent. Eleanora was one of a minuscule number of students she'd ever chosen to see after graduation.

Thus did my father inform me (I would understand it this way only later) that I was on my own but in a place where I must not dishonor my family.

The Stoneparks lived in the building on Park Avenue where Jason had been raised. The rooms were large and pleasant, the walls full of paintings by Jason *or* Eleanora. That is to say, their paintings did not share rooms. Jason's huge oils, hung in the pleasant living room with its big, soft chairs and sofas in shades of teal and gray, were powerful and somber abstracts in black, brown, and gray, easier to describe than to look at, impossible to trace, at least with this viewer's brain, to the gentle soul who took an interest in other humans his wife did not appear to share. On the other hand, it became apparent as I followed him from the living room, through a long hallway with hundreds of family photographs, into a large, bright room hung with Eleanora's paintings which was clearly the place where the family spent most of its time, that what *he* did not share with *her* was a talent for painting wonderful pictures.

The walls, the curtains, and the chair upholstery were all a soft yellow that seemed to provide sunshine even on a day as gray as this one. The floor was covered by a sisal rug. Tall windows looked out on a terrace that ran around two sides of the room. Aside from those windows and their curtains, Eleanora's paintings and sketches were the only objects at eye level or higher.

I'm not sure whether I actually gasped as I entered the room and saw them, or whether memory has me dramatizing a real reaction, but I found them beautiful and wonderful. Along with many watercolors (Later, seeing Chianti country, my first thought was that the landscape was almost as beautiful as it had been in her paintings) were several oils, a few drawings of the (naked) female form, and a couple of portraits of (dressed) men. When I try now to remember specific pictures, I see one vast swirl of brilliant color.

I was standing at the room's entrance, thunderstruck—artstruck, if you will—with Jason just ahead and slightly to one side of me, when I heard a child's voice mimicking an engine's sound, and at the same moment was knocked into Jason by that child as he barged past us into the room, thrusting before him the largest toy engine I'd ever seen.

Jason straightened us out and said, as we watched the boy, who was then eight, circling the room, still making his engine noises, "Well, now you've met Evan, and I'm sure if you've survived at all, you're the better for it . . . You are all right, aren't you?"

"Mmm," I said. "I'm fine, thank you."

My eyes returned to the nearest paintings while my brain wished for a few minutes alone with them before I was required to talk or to deal with Evan. It was not to be.

"Who're you?" the boy asked.

"My name is Caroline," I said.

"Are you my mother's friend or my father's?" he asked.

I replied with a straight face that actually *my* mother and father were friends of *his* mother and father.

"So how come you're the one who's here?" he asked.

Now I allowed myself to smile. "They invited me."

"They must want you to do something," he said. "Are you a good baby-sitter?"

Beside me Jason groaned good-naturedly and without serious concern.

"I don't know if I'm a good one or a bad one because I've never done it," I replied.

"Oh, well," Evan said. "You will if you come to Italy with us."

I turned to Jason and was about to tell him I hoped his invitation wasn't about that because I'd promised my parents I'd go to summer school when Eleanora Stonepark breezed into the room in a flowing black velvet hostess gown of a sort I'd never seen before. Eleanora never wore anything but black, a phenomenon in those days in a way that it isn't now.

I find myself, as I try to describe the condition of my brain at that moment, going to a framed page of Eleanora's ink drawings I would see only later, as we sat at lunch. There was a tree in full leaf and flower. Next to it stood the same tree, recognizable but beginning to break into cubes and other less specific forms. And next to that a mad swirl unrecognizable as the tree in any way you could specify but that you understood to represent its soul.

Eleanora fixed on me one of her more dazzling smiles. (Later I would grade them as Earth and Sky Light Up; Earth Only; The Neighborhood; The Room. Her mouth made the same motions with each of them, yet the range in effect was staggering.) "So," she said, "are we thinking it all might work?"

I stared at her. I had the feeling gates had closed behind me.

"My dear," Jason said, moving to her side, putting a protective arm around her although I was quite certain it was I who required protection, "Caroline has just arrived and I haven't told her about our idea."

"Oh, God," said Eleanora, a model of adorable dismay, "I hope I haven't ruined things."

"You have never in your entire life ruined anything," Jason assured her. "You have simply made it desirable for me to explain why we've invited Caroline to lunch though we don't know her very well." He turned to me. "May I offer you a glass of wine? The food will be ready any moment."

I nodded.

He pressed a buzzer on the wall and a maid appeared. She was asked to bring us some white wine. Eleanora had settled into an easy chair with a copy of *Vogue,* which she was flipping through as though some question had been answered and she could go back to thinking about whatever really concerned her. When the maid brought our wine, Evan said he wanted to have lunch with us. Eleanora, without looking up from her *Vogue,* said in Italian that this didn't seem like a good idea (I don't know if this is the time to mention that Eleanora was an upper-middle-class Jewish girl from Manhattan who was then thirty-eight years old, to her husband's fifty), at which point Jason steered the protesting child into the kitchen.

"Let me tell you about the farmhouse in Gaiole," he said when the three of us had settled at the table. Our first course, prosciutto and melon, was in front of us. "It's an easy drive from Florence and we do it often. We spend as much time as we can at the house, we both have studios right there, and when Evan's on vacation, we're normally there. Our usual help, or at least those of our help who've had the care of Evan, generally accompany us. But now, for a variety of reasons, we'd like to change that. Aside from any other consideration, he hasn't been learning Italian in the natural, you might say, manner we'd hoped he might. In the way you yourself did."

Jason explained that it hadn't occurred to him to look for

someone like me until the night of our dinner, when it had come to seem that each and every problem they had in Italy, beginning with the language matter, going on to the way they liked to eat (the female half of the live-in couple was "a Sicilian with an exceedingly limited repertory," but transporting another cook to and home from the farm was a nuisance, aside from the matter of many Italian women's balking at trying French dishes), and ending with the matter of having someone look after Evan whom he could actually enjoy, might be solved if I would come to Italy with them. This summer was particularly important because Eleanora was having her first major show the following winter and would be working even harder than she usually did.

"Now," Jason said, "you're not even to try to make a decision immediately. You are to think about the possibilities and enjoy your lunch."

But the two were mutually exclusive: Was I allowed to explain about my parents' insistence that I go to summer school to make up for lost time, or would I find out when I reached home that this had been a breach of faith?

In between the melon and prosciutto and our main course, a lovely fish salad I could barely choke down, Eleanora began sketching, using a piece of paper from a pile and a pencil from a mug filled with sharp ones that rested on top of it near her place at the table. A couple of times I thought I felt her glancing at me and as we ate (Periodically she put down her fork and sketched for a moment) I became convinced that I was her subject. My indecision about how to find out was made keener by the fact that there was very little conversation about anything, and no apparent sense, on anyone else's part, of something missing.

I had grown up at a table where four active academics reviewed aloud what they were doing, frequently with a sense of competition and/or urgency. Now, with my sister and brother gone, my parents discussed whatever concerned the two of them. I knew many details of their current grant proposals, geared to their eagerness to go together to Japan: My mother wanted to study the influence of Japanese art on Impressionism between the two World Wars; my father's proposal had to do with relations between Germany and Japan. Here, Eleanora's very presence made table chat superfluous, although Jason volunteered an occasional comment or offered me food.

I contained myself until I'd finished my fish salad but then I leaned over to see what was on her paper.

"You have a good face," Eleanora said. "I'd love to paint you some time." She smiled winsomely, turning around the paper to show me a pencil sketch instantly recognizable as the Real Me.

I was dumbstruck.

"She's upset by my picture," Eleanora said gravely to Jason.

"Oh, no," I croaked, gasped, "It's wonderful! I can't believe you just . . ."

She had *seen* me in some way that my parents, never mind my parents, *my best friends* did not. I was viewed by my friends as easy to get along with. It was my enjoyable peculiarity to be interested in what girls had once *thought* they were interested in—most particularly, of course, in cooking. My friends' mothers had gone to Barnard, Vassar, and Radcliffe then married, learned to cook, read good books, and joined the PTA. Their daughters, whether because they'd been galvanized by the new Women's Movement or because they had some specific interest, intelligence, and/or drive, wanted to be lawyers (mostly), doctors (practicing down South or serving in the Peace Corps), or, in one case, to run for Congress. When we had group sleepovers, I cooked. If they apologized for putting me to work, I told them I didn't mind. But saying I didn't mind had nothing to do with being *agreeable;* it was the *truth*. I found the preparation of the food as compelling as the gossip, which I also enjoyed. Because the other girls did not share my pleasure in cooking, they attributed my willingness to virtue.

Eleanora Stonepark, in the most casual way imaginable, had seen my dark side. The face she'd drawn was of a quirky and difficult human being whose mouth had a distinctly sardonic turn—as my fleshly one did not. At the same time, the flaws in the person she had portrayed, perhaps because that person seemed intelligent and self-possessed, were tolerable to me in a way that the flaws in her model were not.

After lunch, Eleanora picked up the piece of paper with my soul on it and appeared to be about to leave the table.

"May I have it?" I asked without debating whether it was acceptable to do this. My voice trembled and I was sure that I would cry if she said no, while I could not imagine why she would want to hold on to it.

"Of course you may," Eleanora said graciously. "But first . . . I want to play with it for a while, you know?"

I nodded, mesmerized.

"What I think," she said, suddenly winsome, playful, "is that by the time we've had our lovely summer, I'll be ready to part with it. For all I know, I'll have done a painting, by then."

I could barely breathe.

"You don't understand," I gasped. "I'd *love* to go to Gaiole." I probably would have wanted to go even without this cleverly mounted bait. Whether it was a judgment about her work or a reaction to her presence, or both, I had been conquered by Eleanora Stonepark, a woman who could do something extraordinary and wonderful that no one else I knew could do. And then, of course, there was Jason, a moderate and easy person who would always be around if Eleanora's artistic temperament or my own somewhat anti-authoritarian bias should pose any problems.

"I just *can't.* I promised my parents I'd go to summer school."

"Are you telling us," Eleanora asked gravely, "that the only thing standing between you and a summer in Gaiole is your parents?"

I nodded.

Eleanora, who understood better than I her power over my parents, not to say over me and various others, smiled.

That evening my parents began the conversation that would end in my receiving permission to go to Gaiole by saying that they understood the only thing preventing me from working for the Stoneparks was their own "perhaps foolish" insistence that I push through six credits in school, and ended it by extracting a promise from me—as though I'd pleaded with them to go—to work harder than I otherwise would have during the term that followed.

This is not a story about my summer with the Stoneparks, which, if it wasn't always easy, was tolerable for a variety of reasons.

Gaiole was hot but very beautiful and there was a large pool on the land in back of the house. (Most of the vineyard was on a hillside across a winding dirt road, the road that led to the *autostrada* on which we drove to Florence.) The household was run around Eleanora's preparation for her show. (It was understood that Jason was not under similar pressure, but unless I'm mistaken, there was always some reason for the house's being run around Eleanora.) It worked because most of her time was spent in the studio. My primary job was to keep Evan out of her way when he wasn't with his father. This became easier as Evan forgot about my being a hired hand and came actually to enjoy my company.

My absorption in the physical matter of everyday life made it easier in a variety of ways for me to get along with Eleanora. When I was challenged about food (or almost anything else), I became intent upon solving the problem. This also worked with Evan, who got hooked into kitchen matters and began to learn Italian from me very much as I had learned it from Anna. Finally, I was fascinated by the operation of the vineyard, and my fascination led to a very agreeable affair with Angelo Ferrante, who managed that vineyard and several others owned by non-residents. (The Stoneparks' had its own beautiful label, designed by Eleanora. Framed in gold and printed in brilliant colors, its central image was a goblet of red wine standing on a rock in front of a green shrub.)

Angelo, a lively-homely man of thirty-one given to pronouncements like, "All American girls are spoiled"—always in Italian, of course—had a wife and five children in Sicily, and was casually flirtatious but became friendly when I spoke a non-touristy Italian he could readily understand. (He had English but wouldn't use it.) Our affair began less than two weeks after I'd arrived at the beginning of June, but our friendship commenced on the day I told him, in Italian, of course, that he should not judge all American women by Eleanora Stonepark.

Angelo stopped in his tracks. We'd been walking between two rows of vines set on the big old tree branches that were his favorite stakes. He turned to me, hands on hips, and said something that translates as, "Ah, finally! I thought there must be something wrong with you, that you never complain about the bitch!"

I felt more defensive than conspiratorial—yet, oddly, it was Eleanora, not myself, I felt compelled to defend, with a little speech about how artists couldn't be held to the same standard as the rest of us. This infuriated Angelo, who said that artist or no artist, he'd kick the shit out of me if I ever acted like that.

I don't want to convey the impression that I precisely *liked* Eleanora, whose behavior was very much that of the royal personage. But my sense of her as an artist whose work gave me great pleasure dominated my reactions, muted them when required. She was the way artists were *supposed* to be. And then of course there was my powerful desire, never voiced but with me every day of my life in Gaiole, to own the promised drawing or—too much really to hope for—the painting she might choose to do.

Whether because veneration prevented me from getting angry at otherwise insufferable words and deeds, or because of the convenience Evan's attachment to me afforded, or because of my increasing skill at cooking Italian haute cuisine, or because I didn't happen to have any of the habits that got under Eleanora's skin and turned her into a screeching lunatic (talking a lot, saying *gezundheit* or God bless you when someone sneezed, and spending more than a few seconds gnawing the meat remaining on bones when most had been cut off are crimes I remember offhand), Eleanora's behavior toward me was very much the same when we reached the middle of August as it had been in June.

It had been understood when I took the job that I would leave Gaiole a week before the family did to register for my classes. As the time for my departure drew close, Angelo grew melancholy over the prospect of my disappearance, *la mia sparizione.* An early member of the first generation of females more scared of falling in love than of getting pregnant, I had assured myself, the first time I allowed him to show me an absent neighbor's villa, that it was OK to go to bed because I wasn't going to fall in love with him. Now, as he pressed me to delay my leavetaking, I was finding that whether or not you called it love, if you liked it, you didn't want it to end.

Jason had taken Evan into town on some errand. Angelo and I were lying on a tarp at the far end of the vineyard. The sunset was particularly beautiful and the aroma of ripening grapes filled the air. I told him that I didn't actually have to be at school until the end of that week and he said he had business in Sicily, we could drive down the coast together. He would bring me to the airport down there. Nobody (Nobody was always Eleanora, whose name he was loathe to pronounce) would even have to know. He would exchange my ticket, which Jason had already given me. I could tell the Stoneparks that he, Angelo, was taking me to the airport. He began immediately to plan for our trip to Palermo, where he had wine business. He'd always said that Sicily was *un altro mondo,* and it was a world I had to see.

I did not mention our trip in explaining to Jason that I wouldn't require transportation to the airport. Attempting to avoid a direct lie, I said something like, "Angelo is going to drive me." Jason simply nodded, but that evening, which was a week before the date I was scheduled to leave, Eleanora joined Jason, Evan, and me for dinner for the first time in days.

I had been wondering more and more whether she remembered about my picture, and if so, whether she would give it to me. I had a strong enough sense of her to know that I was best off not being the one to raise the issue; nothing riled Eleanora more than the suggestion of an act outside forces required her to perform. But I also knew that I was not going to leave without making a strong effort to get what I'd been promised. (I spent a great deal of time trying to decide which I'd prefer, the drawing or a watercolor. In one fantasy, she gave me both because she was so pleased with my summer's work. In another, she painted a marvelous portrait, parting with it reluctantly because she loved it—me—so much.)

Eleanora, a master of psychology when it might effect some improvement in her life, spent a lot of time praising the green soup I'd made the day before, yawning, and telling us that no matter how exhausted she was, she simply had to go back to work after dinner, she couldn't believe she had only two weeks left in Gaiole. Jason ate doggedly during this monologue but at some point he put down his soup spoon. He looked perturbed. He did not meet my eyes—or Eleanora's.

"I'm not sure which upsets me more," Eleanora said, looking directly at me for the first time since she'd begun, "my having to leave in two weeks or your leaving in one."

Evan looked up from his soup. "One? One? What do you mean, leaving in one?"

I smiled uncomfortably. "I thought your parents must have told you already," I said. "I have to be in school the week before you do."

"I am the guilty party," Eleanora announced bravely as Evan looked from her to his father and back. "It was too awful. I didn't even remind myself and I certainly never thought to tell anyone. Not that I've been able to think about anything except the paintings. I don't have three-quarters . . . No, that's not true . . . I'm lying to myself . . . I don't have *half* the number of pictures I promised Bruce and Leon. I really don't know what I'm going to do." Her eyes brimmed with tears and her voice shook.

In what might have been the masterstroke of his entire childhood, Evan picked this moment not only to deliver a monologue that was at once a tribute to me and a threat about his behavior when/if I left, but to do it *in Italian,* which he normally refused to employ when his parents were around, but saved for the time when we were alone. Weeks earlier I had given Jason permission to spy on us to determine that this was true. Not only was it true, but I was aware that Evan occasionally looked up words to save as surprises. He had developed a crush on me, and I had a more difficult day if he happened to see me talking to Angelo.

"I don't believe this is happening now," he declaimed in

patchy but adequate Italian. "Tell me you're kidding around. Tell me the plans I've made don't have to be thrown away. All the things we wanted to do that we didn't have time for . . . All the . . . And I can't believe you didn't even *tell* me!"

"I thought you knew, love," I responded, also in Italian. "And I have to tell you, I'm impressed with your vocabulary, and I bet your folks are, too."

"Impressed! Impressed!" Eleanora said dramatically. "But what good will it do if you're not here to talk with him?"

This was classic Eleanora, unable to imagine a use for his Italian, now that he had it, beyond keeping him busy and out of her way. I started to respond, if only for Evan's sake, saying I thought it would do a great deal of good because he enjoyed it, as witness the vocabulary he had, which meant he was—when Eleanora interrupted to ask me on which day I was actually required to register and Evan went around the table to sit on his father's lap.

I stopped dead in my verbal tracks, unable to answer because I hadn't thought out a lie and the truth would tell her I had an extra few days I could choose to remain.

"The truth is," I lied, "I don't exactly remember. I think it's the fourth, but—"

"Would you like to call home and ask?" Eleanora interrupted.

"Uh, no, uh, not really," I said. "I mean, even if it's a couple of days later, I need some time to get myself organized, buy some clothes, that kind of thing."

I looked at Jason, who was toying with his piece of bread, embarrassed, I believe, at what his wife was doing to me. Which didn't mean he was about to jump in on my side, a reality I was mulling over even as Eleanora began to speak.

"Well, I was just thinking . . . I have to admit I was thinking about it because Jason mentioned your leaving, and I was looking at that little sketch of you, you know, I have it on the bulletin board over my drafting table . . . Or maybe you don't . . . I don't know how recently you've been in the studio . . ." (I had been in the studio once at the beginning of the summer but had not been invited again.) "Anyway, what I was thinking was about how I meant to do a little watercolor portrait, you were so pleased with the sketch, and now I won't have time to do it."

I thought—I might have imagined it because it's so perfect but I don't actually believe I did—I thought I saw Jason blush, although he didn't look up. Perhaps if he hadn't been a witness I would have caved in at that moment, promised to stay if Eleanora would do the watercolor. Evan was looking back and forth between us, not commenting on the transaction, which he already understood to be just that, and one in which his interests coincided with his mother's.

"How's Angelo?" she asked.

My breath was taken away. It was the first time she'd ever so much as mentioned Angelo, who dealt only with Jason.

"He seems to be fine," I said stiffly.

"Is Angelo the reason you don't need us to take you to the airport?" she asked.

"Yes," I said, trying to figure out what I would do if she asked any more questions.

She was smart enough not to. After a pause, she pushed away her plates, set both elbows on the table, her chin on her hands. "OK. Here's the deal I have to offer. Stay till we go and I'll do the watercolor."

I couldn't breathe, much less cry, though I had a strong desire to do both. Something prevented me from caving in right away. I turned to Evan and told him that no matter what I decided, I cared about him and would stay in touch when we were all in New York. Eleanora's words were repeating themselves in my head, and when I had delivered this message to him, I turned back to his mother.

"You said you'd do it," I pointed out. "You didn't say it would be mine."

She smiled. "My goodness, love, you've gotten so suspicious. Of course it will be yours. I'm only doing it for you."

Note the tense; if I did not assume she would have her way, Eleanora already did. And of course she'd forgotten her original notion that my face was too fascinating *not* to paint.

The stumbling block was Angelo. While I wanted the painting even more than I wanted to drive south with him, I was scared of his reaction when I told him I couldn't go. With Jason's permission, I called my parents, who would be leaving for Japan in between the time I'd been supposed to arrive and the time I would if I stayed, to ask if one of them would register for me if I remained in Gaiole until the Stoneparks left. It is fair to say they were happier to do it for this reason than they would have been for another. Then I told Eleanora that I would remain if she would give me the picture before that extra week arrived. Until then, I would hold on to the ticket Jason had already given me, for the earlier flight out of Florence.

"Trusting little soul, aren't you," Eleanora commented, at once pleased by her work's importance to me and irritated by the doubt that was implicit in my condition.

"I trust," I said calmly (I'd been preparing the line from the moment I awakened that morning), "that your work is the most important thing to you and that you'll do whatever you have to do to keep it going."

She let out a hearty laugh, and slammed a hand down on the table.

"Is that the one you had waiting?" she asked. "Is that why Jason got Evan out of here?"

In fact, Evan was angry with me, which was why he had chosen to go to the tennis court with Jason. I'd explained to him about school and about how the whole arrangement had been made before I even really *knew* him and had nothing to do with anything but preparing for school, but my explanation hadn't altered his feelings. That evening, when Eleanora had capitulated, telling me that if I wasn't "too busy," I should visit her studio in the evening, I told Evan I hoped to be able to remain with him in Gaiole until the end, after all. He became provisionally friendly without displaying any interest in how or why this had been arranged. Informed that we were all set, he became affectionate again.

Angelo was even less easily mollified, my explanation of why I could not go down the coast being greeted by an extraordinary diatribe punctuated by references to secrets he hadn't told me yet that he would have revealed on the trip and curses I hadn't learned yet but could identify as such. It was only when he expressed incredulity that I should care about anything done by that *puttana,* and I told him maybe *I* was the whore because her paintings were worth big money in the States (a lie I didn't yet know would turn into the truth), that his rage diminished and he became interested in the matter of what her work was worth.

At nine o'clock, when Evan had gone to his room with his father, I walked around the grounds for a few minutes, then went into the house and upstairs to the back, which faced north and held Eleanora's studio. (Jason's faced south. He was said not to mind the summer heat or to need the northern light preferred by painters.) I knocked twice and waited for what seemed like a very long time until she called to me to enter. I did so.

It was a breathtaking room, even at night, when the glass wall at its far end was no longer letting in the entire countryside and all the (indirect) light in the world. Eleanora's unfinished paintings were propped against the otherwise bare walls, giving the lie to her suggestion that she worked on only one at a time. Finished works stood in racks against one wall. Her easel and worktable were near the window. She sat at the former, facing it and nearly invisible to me.

"Sit down," she ordered. "I'll be with you in a minute."

Was she going to make a great show, I wondered, of rushing to finish the painting she really *should* be working on in order to deal with my selfish demands? I decided I couldn't anticipate all the possibilities and simply had to remain firm. My terms were my terms. I relaxed somewhat into this posture and spent my waiting time admiring the unfinished pictures, surreptitiously watching her work, wondering what she was painting. It's probably easy to imagine how I felt when after perhaps fifteen or twenty minutes, her left hand came around the easel to beckon to me, and I walked, nearly on tiptoe, to the easel, and she brought me around to stand beside her, and I was looking at a delicate and still-damp watercolor that had obviously begun in the pencil sketch of me.

I gasped.

There I was. My straight brown hair, my murky brown-green eyes, the blue turtleneck sweater I'd worn to their house for lunch months earlier and hadn't worn since but which she'd apparently remembered as she apparently remembered every visual detail she'd once taken in, and, most importantly, the sense of her subject's power that had first captivated me, perhaps even more emphatic than it had been in the drawing.

I couldn't have minded less. That is to say, if she had been looking for a little revenge upon the youngster who was extracting a price, she'd failed to find it. In any event, I doubt she could have made me look bad enough to anger me and I don't believe she'd actually tried. Her artistic conscience, surely the strongest of any of the kinds of conscience she might have possessed, would not have allowed her to turn me into anyone substantially more monstrous than I was. I prepared to have her hand me the painting and wave me out of the room, but if I was already more than satisfied with the work, she was not. I sat for more than an hour as she painted and fussed and finally, when she'd announced that she was finished and I, with tears in my eyes, had told her it was wonderful, she promised to look in the attic the next morning for a frame that fit. I could have it in the evening.

I did.

I had it and I treasured it. Even if the summer had been far more difficult, possessing my picture would have made it worthwhile. When we all went to Florence that weekend for our farewell visit to Evan's favorite restaurant, I picked up a large, touristy satchel whose sole virtue was that it would safely hold the painting (between two pieces of corrugated board) during the trip home. On the plane I sat stiffly with the bag in back of me, the corrugated board cushioned in turn by laundry on both sides. I was unwilling to put it under the seat in front lest it slide away. Reaching home (my parents had left two days earlier), I decided to return to the big bedroom that had once been mine and use the maid's room for my guests. The apparent reason was that, with my parents gone, most of the apartment was unoccupied. The real reason was that, fond as I was of the little room, it had no wall that could do justice to my painting.

I hung it so that it faced me as I lay in my bed in the big room. Had it been feasible, I would have removed not only all other decoration but the two narrow bookcases standing against that wall. I did set them as far as possible from one another. The portrait of the interesting human being perceived by Eleanora Stonepark hung solitary, nearly regal, between them. It would not be exaggerating to say that although I didn't think about her all the time, the world scared me less when she was with me than it did when I was alone. She was my promise that somewhere inside me there was a real person who might someday do something interesting.

I'd returned to school the previous year because it was my side of an agreement, not because academia had come to seem more inviting. I felt alienated from the younger students by what I'd learned out in the real world, but I lacked the desire to pass on reality's wisdom (Dope or no dope there were dishes to be washed, and so on). With all the time I'd spent congratulating myself on not thinking that I was in love with Angelo, I was dismayed to find, as I walked around the campus looking at scraggly-haired Jewish suburbanites and Midwestern blonds who rolled reefers as easily as they'd once caught pop flies, that I missed him more than I'd dreamed I might in the days when I was giving up his company to acquire my painting.

Not that I ever regretted the exchange. It was, after all, my future self, as revealed to me by Eleanora's painting, who assured me of being a real person with interests I would develop, if only I were allowed to do so. In fact, at some point during the autumn it occurred to me that it was no coincidence that the person who had portrayed me as an interesting human being was also a person who seriously appreciated my cooking.

I began to daydream about attending the Culinary Institute in upstate New York, a fantasy that seemed a little more realistic than the notion of getting my parents to pay my tuition at one of the great cooking schools in France. Eventually the very possession of a daydream about something I wanted to do diminished my sense of being empty and uninteresting enough to allow me to make a few new friends.

Perhaps it's simplest for me to quote the letter from the Root-Pierson Gallery, dated November 21st of that year, in its entirety.

Dear Miss Weiss:

As you probably know, the Root-Pierson Gallery is planning an exhibition of the paintings of Eleanora Stonepark to open in New York on January 1st of next year and, after a month here, to travel to Boston and Washington.

We understand from Mrs. Stonepark that you own one of her few watercolor portraits, *116th Street Jenny,* which we would like to include in the exhibition. We would need to have it in the gallery by December 20th. We would, of course, take care of all transportation and insurance costs.

We very much look forward to hearing from you, at which time we will send the Gallery's formal loan agreement. And of course we hope you will attend the opening. Eleanora Stonepark will be present. We will be sending you the announcement and invitation at a later date.

Sincerely,
Bruce Pierson

It took me very little time to frame my response:

Dear Mr. Pierson:

I have your letter asking me to lend you my picture. I am sorry that I cannot do this.

Sincerely,
Caroline Weiss

There was no question of my being willing to risk the kind of damage that might be done to my precious picture.

I hesitated only over the matter of explaining my need to live with the person I did not and never would think of as 116th Street Jenny. But the phrases that came to my mind when I considered such an explanation were at once so precise and so melodramatic ("I'm sorry, I can't live without her, she is my promise of a future") that I decided to forgo an explanation.

At the beginning of the school term Evan had called, wanting me to spend that Saturday afternoon with him. I'd been unable to do this. When I'd called him a couple of Saturdays later because I had some time, Jason had told me Evan was visiting a friend. He went on to say that they thought of me often and felt the summer had been very good for Evan. I'd not talked to either father or son since then, but now I had a call from Jason. The matter of lending the painting had left my mind completely once my letter was mailed, and when I heard his voice, I assumed he was calling because I had failed to do so.

"Hi," I said, "I want you to know, it's not that I haven't been thinking about him, but I'm so busy, and when you said he was getting along, I guess I just . . ."

"I wasn't actually calling about Evan," Jason said. "I was calling about the business of lending the painting."

"Oh, yes," I said quickly, still far from understanding the nature of the ground I was treading upon. "I can understand why they want it, but . . . If anyone knows how much I love it, how important it is to me . . ."

"Yes, of course," Jason said. "That was why Eleanora gave it to you. She could see how you felt about the work."

I did not awaken to the gravity of the matter. Nor did it occur to me to point out that her motives had been somewhat more complex and selfish than he was suggesting.

"Mmm," I said. "I mean, I love all her stuff, but then there's the business of . . . I mean, she *saw* me, you know?

I never felt as though anyone knew who I was, I didn't know *myself,* and then Eleanora *saw* me."

"Ah, yes," Jason said after a moment. "Well, what she's seeing at the moment is a young woman who won't lend her back her own painting when she needs it desperately for a show."

Now I heard him. It did not cross my mind that I should part with my portrait, but I realized, finally, that my refusal was not a simple matter.

"I don't," I began after a while, "I don't . . ." My voice cracked. I had no way to finish the sentence. For the first time since they'd gone overseas, I wished desperately that my parents were home. Maybe they'd have come to my aid, explained to Jason better than I could how the painting . . . I began to cry, covering the receiver so he would not hear me.

"Caroline?" he said after a moment. "Are you there?"

"Yes," I said, sobbing.

"Can you tell me . . . Are you afraid you won't get it back at the end of the show?"

I was afraid of not surviving its absence, but I knew this was crazy and I mustn't say it.

"What I really . . . It's the only thing on the wall. The wall will be . . . I mean, I look at it all the time. She's *with* me. I can't imagine . . . I mean, it's a very long time, Jason." Until then the difference between three days and three months had seemed unimportant. Without realizing it, I had begun to bargain. "You know, I only took the job because I loved her work so much."

"Well," Jason said after a long pause, "what if we gave you one of Eleanora's sketches to keep on the wall while we had the painting?"

"Gave me?" I repeated moronically. "Sketches?"

He misunderstood, thought me in better command than I was of the conversation's content and bargaining for a better offer.

"I'd offer you another watercolor, but the whole problem is that there are only a few watercolors Eleanora feels are good enough for the show, and there's no other portrait, and she hasn't been working in watercolor, and she usually works very slowly, that painting was a freak, in a sense, and she's particularly fond of it. She didn't want to let go of it when she finished, but she never would have dreamed of failing to honor her part of your bargain."

Particularly since I wouldn't have stayed the extra week if she hadn't.

The thought passed through my brain but once again made no effort to drop into my mouth. In fact, I was silent as I tried to absorb what he was saying and understand what it meant to me and my portrait. Jason, a sophisticated slave to the Empress Eleanora, waited for me to grasp the magnitude of what she had done for me, the ignominious nature of my response.

"I'm sorry," I finally said, not apologizing but expressing regret at the difficulty of our situation.

"Well," Jason said, "I accept your apology, but of course you haven't accepted my solution to our problem."

My problem was his telephone call, which I wanted desperately to be finished with.

"I have an idea," Jason said in a different, perhaps artificially hearty voice. "I think you and I should go to Eleanora's studio, where you'll be able to look at her sketches and the paintings that won't be in the show and find one you'd like to put in Jenny's place. How does that sound?"

"OK," I managed to say after a very long time in which my brain hadn't accepted the notion, but had come to understand I had to go along with it.

"All right, then," Jason said. "There's someone waiting for me and I have to go, now, but I'll be in touch in a day or two. Bye."

I said good-bye and hung up, then returned to my room, stretched out on the bed, looked at my picture, and gradually allowed my saner self to come into control of my brain. Loving the picture didn't mean I had to see it every day of my life. I loved people I didn't see for years at a time and then, there they were again, and it was just as it had been before. If I missed my girl (Her name was not and never would be Jenny, damn it, much less the demeaning 116th Street Jenny; if I'd had to be given a name other than Caroline, at least I might have been consulted) terribly, I could visit the gallery . . . at least the one in New York. And it wasn't as though I would miss her because of a space on the wall. Someone—or something—would be there, keeping her place for her and for me. I could almost feel good about Jason's solution. Certainly I could wish it had come more easily. In any event, it would be exciting, to visit Eleanora's studio. I could almost look forward to hearing from Jason.

But two days later there was another letter from Bruce Pierson that made me regret having opened myself to the whole idea.

Dear Miss Weiss:

This is to confirm your telephone conversation with Jason Stonepark in which you agreed that you would go to Mrs. Stonepark's studio to select a substitute for the watercolor you will lend to the Root-Pierson Gallery's exhibition of her work, January 1st through March 31st.

We have enclosed a loan form which we ask you to return to us as soon as possible so the pick-up can be arranged. Thanks so much for your cooperation in this matter.

Sincerely,
Bruce Pierson

I was as angry as though I'd never agreed to the substitution plan. Did they really believe I was going to turn over my painting and then sit around waiting for a phone call? What kind of an idiot did they think I was? Even if Eleanora Stonepark hadn't been a difficult and duplicitous human being, Jason a subservient one who would say anything to appease her, I would have been a fool to consent to such an arrangement. I sat down and fired off a letter to Pierson that I can't bear to quote here, but which began with the suggestion that they were treating me not only like a child, but a dumb one, and ended by saying there were no circumstances under which I would permit my painting to leave and I didn't want to hear from any of them again.

I did not.

Eleanora's show opened to great acclaim, remained open for a month in New York, closed. I paid little attention. I was determined to do enough schoolwork so my parents wouldn't claim I'd failed to keep my side of our bargain, and I had a reasonable social life by this time. When my summer money had run out, I'd taken a four-night-a-week baby-sitting job with a neighborhood mother, Jackie Liebman, a working divorcée who was attending night school. I got along with Jackie as well as with her children (she couldn't get over the fact that I happily cooked meals and baked bread and cookies with the children) and in the spring, she told me she and some friends had rented a house on Fire Island for the summer and needed a responsible housekeeper-babysitter. I explained that I would be in summer school but could make a weekend—perhaps even a three- or four-day weekend arrangement. Jackie found someone who would take the other days until the week in August when I finished school. That week coincided with my parents' return from Japan. I did not see them, although we spoke on the phone, until I returned to New York with the Liebmans after Labor Day.

They were pleased with the way I'd kept the apartment,

satisfied with what I told them of school, and glad I'd found a job that did not interfere with my schoolwork. (I would return to part-time baby-sitting for Jackie.) I judged them unready for a conversation about cooking school, nor did I have any reason to rush. I had applied to the Culinary Institute of America but knew there were far more applications than there were places and I was far from certain I'd be admitted. They admired Eleanora's painting and exclaimed over her generosity in having given it to me. I told them I'd made a deal with her, but the story of the deal, briefly told, appeared not to alter their vision of her virtue, and I could not make myself tell them what had happened later. My natural reluctance combined with the obligations accumulated during their year in the Orient to delay the day of reckoning.

Then, on a Sunday evening in late autumn, when my father and I were reading *The Times* in the living room, my mother came in with a funny expression on her face and, leaning against the wall next to the entrance, asked, "What happened with the Stoneparks?"

Startled, terribly anxious, I tried to remember what I'd decided to say when this question arose. All I could think of was my father's telling me, a zillion years ago, what a high opinion my mother had of Eleanora.

"The Stoneparks," I repeated.

My father looked up.

"What happened . . . basically . . . is . . . they wanted my painting."

"*Your* painting?" my mother said. "You mean *her* painting that she was so extraordinarily generous as to give you?"

"She wasn't exactly being generous," I said, feeling the muddy water come up around my eyes. "We made a deal where she would give it to me if—"

"Did you or did you not refuse to let her borrow her own painting for her show?"

I nodded. This was going to be even worse than I'd feared. My mother's eyes closed and her body—could it be my imagination?—sagged. After a moment she felt her way along the wall to the nearest chair, a stiff-backed uncomfortable job she occasionally piled magazines on but that none of us ever sat in. My father had put down his newspaper.

"I didn't exactly refuse," I said. "At least I wasn't *going* to. I mean, I was, then I wasn't, and then I got this awful letter." They were staring at me in horror. I had begun to plead. "You don't know what went on with that painting. You don't know what I went through to get it. It was the only reason I took the job in the first place, she sort of promised it, and then when I finally got it, I mean, I had to stay an extra week and not take a trip I wanted to take and then I only—"

"Maybe," my father said, "you had better bring us the letter."

"Letters," I corrected automatically.

"Letters," he said.

My mother's eyes were still closed. Her mouth trembled. I went to my room, finding the correspondence easily since it wasn't with all the stuff I kept on the top of my desk because I might need to look at it again. Now I could see that was wishful thinking. I was going to have to make clear the extent of the picture's importance to me; it wasn't just the idea of the promise, I cared about the *picture*. If they didn't understand that, they'd never forgive me for angering their friends. They'd kick me out of the house before I ever mentioned the Culinary Institute!

I returned to the living room. They were sitting together on the sofa, my father's arm around my mother. They looked as though they'd come from a funeral.

"There's something I want to explain before I give you the letters," I said.

"You can explain later," my father said.

I handed them over. He did not look at me, nor did my mother. I turned to leave the room and was ordered, in a voice I'd seldom heard, to sit down. I sat in the chair my mother had used earlier and waited, trying, with only limited success, to breathe.

"Oh, my God," was the only thing my mother said—so quickly that I thought there must be some mistake.

When they had finished, they looked up at me. They appeared to be considerably more astonished than John Hinckley's parents would be, some years later, upon learning of their son's attempt to kill Ronald Reagan.

"What on earth possessed you?" my mother asked, her voice breaking. "How could you possibly . . ." But she trailed off, failing to find the words to describe so heinous a crime.

"That's what I was trying to explain," I said. "I couldn't imagine doing without it. I hardly had it on the wall when they wanted it back and I couldn't . . ." My voice broke as I pleaded for understanding. "I love her. It. I couldn't imagine parting with her. She was my company when I was alone here. I—"

"Of *course* you love it," my mother broke in. "Of *course* you . . ." But she was still unable to cope with the enormity of my offense and once again, her words trailed off.

"The issue is not whether you love the painting," my father said. "The issue is whether you have the right to refuse an artist the chance to show her own work."

I was silenced. In truth, my brain hadn't framed it that way at any point. It didn't change the way I felt about Eleanora or the painting but it gave me something to think about. In truth, I hadn't thought of it as hers but as my own. What my father was saying was that even if it was *my* painting, it was *her* work. It had become mine without ever ceasing to be hers.

"Well," he finally said, "as long as we're having this painful conversation, you might as well tell us your version of the story so we can figure out what we can possibly say to Eleanora."

With some difficulty, I told them about the summer, reminding them of that first Sunday, when I'd come home dazzled by the sketch she'd promised me. I said that dealing with Eleanora had been the most difficult part of my job but I hadn't minded because of my respect for her as an artist. I told them about the friend I'd made in Gaiole who was going to show me southern Italy and how, as I planned to leave exactly when I'd said before I consented to take the job that I had to leave, she had bribed me with the picture to stay.

"But you didn't have to leave," my mother interrupted. "You said you were going to take a trip with your friend."

"That's not the issue," my father said wearily. "Let's stay with the issue."

I was no longer certain what the issue was, but I proceeded with the stuff I'd been sure of before this matter of who owned a painting had arisen, my tale of the imperious Eleanora and the servant who wanted to please because she valued the reward.

"All right," my father finally said. "So, you made your bargain and you got your picture. Eleanora kept her side of your bargain."

"I got the picture first. I was afraid—"

"Yes, yes." He waved a hand in the air. "You told us about all that. You hung your picture. And then you got the letter from Bruce Pierson. You did not understand, I gather, that it is the overriding custom to give an artist back her own work whenever she wants to show it. I have never until now heard of anyone's refusing such a request."

I hung my head in shame. Tears rolled down my cheeks and dropped onto my cotton T-shirt.

"So, you wrote your unacceptable letter, saying you could not do this, at which point Pierson spoke to Jason, who called you and made the extraordinarily generous offer to let you have something else while this was in the show."

"I accepted!" I pointed out eagerly. "I was going to do it. Jason said he'd bring me to the studio, and I could choose something to stay in its place, something she didn't need for the show, and I was still miserable about parting with my picture, but I was going to do it!"

"And then?"

"And then I got the letter."

"This one." My father held up Pierson's letter saying that after I'd signed the form, my painting would be picked up.

I nodded.

"And?"

"Look at it!" I pleaded. "I promise to give them my picture as soon as they want it and all they promise is that at some later date I'll receive a call and go to the studio! They could have taken the picture the next day and let me replace it a week before the show got back! I could have had a bare wall for months! I wasn't sure I'd ever get it back!"

My father was looking at the correspondence again. My mother was staring at me as though trying to figure out how she'd managed, for all these years, not to notice the degree of monstrousness of the creature to whom she'd given birth.

"The loan agreement," my father said, "specifies a pick-up/delivery date of December 22nd or 23rd, that is, a week before the show opens, and a return date of two or three days after it returns to New York. Why should you think for a moment that they wouldn't honor it?"

I stared at him, thunderstruck. Whatever he was reading was utterly foreign to me. It wasn't that I'd forgotten. I'd never seen it! Was it possible I'd never even looked at the agreement that came with the letter? Yes, I had to admit, not only was it possible, but I could almost remember slamming down the letter and the papers stapled to it without a glance at anything past the first page.

"Why do you look so surprised?" my father asked. Beside him, my mother, her arms wrapped around herself, keened like a captain's wife upon hearing that the ship has gone down. "Is it possible that you never even bothered to look at the agreement?"

"Bothered isn't right," I cried out—before crying in. "It wasn't about *bothering*." I hadn't even looked at the contract but had been relieved to have an excuse—an arbitrariness to the letter—to go back on my promise to Jason. "It's that I freaked when I thought about it, and when I read the letter, I just . . . It was as though . . . I couldn't let someone like that have me. I mean, the picture of me!"

My mother, unable to tolerate this babble, stood up and walked out of the living room. My father sat, shaking his head, looking down at the papers in his hand and then back at me as though some new indictment of my behavior had presented itself and he needed only to find a way to frame it. Finally he stood, walked over to me holding the papers in his hand like a hangman's noose, and handed them to me.

"I can only hope," he said, "that you have a somewhat better understanding of the trust involved in holding an artist's work than you did before. Not that I have reason to believe it will help. Our friendship with Eleanora is probably lost, and it would be difficult to exaggerate how painful that will be for us if it turns out to be true. You might want to try writing her a letter, now that you realize what they had every right to expect of you. If you decide to write, you'd better show me the letter before you send it."

Who could tell what I, a monster of no sensibility, might say to further offend the Lady Eleanora? There was no danger, in any event, of my writing to her. If I'd been told I would have to leave home if I failed to write, I think I would have returned to my room and packed my bags instead of locking the door, throwing myself down on the bed and crying, as I did, until I fell asleep. I don't know what I dreamed, but I remember quite precisely the moment when, having slowly awakened and gradually pulled myself together just enough to get up and head for the bathroom, I realized that I had walked past my picture—*the* picture—without once looking in its direction. That is to say, I had looked at the floor to make sure I would *not* see it.

Gradually, over a period of months, Jenny ceased to cause me pain when I glanced her way. But I could not recapture the pleasure of looking. Where once I'd played games with her—peeking, for example, to see if her eyes followed me when I walked across the room, as the Mona Lisa's eyes were said to follow one—now she was just there, like a lot of other people. 116th Street Jenny. If she was the person I would become, it was ridiculous to have assumed that I would like that person. I would live with her the way one lived with, or at least dealt with, a lot of people one wasn't crazy about.

Life went on. Gradually my parents became civil, then casual, and finally friendly enough so that I didn't skitter into my bedroom at every free moment but might hang around for some conversation or a meal. The process was assisted immeasurably when my mother published a monograph from a lecture on women artists she had given at Columbia in which she claimed there was no painter on the American scene more talented than Eleanora Stonepark. I could not swear that it was only after the monograph's publication in *Art News* that the two couples became friendly again. I do know it was then that the name Stonepark (as in Dinner 8-Stoneparks) began to appear on the calendar hanging on the refrigerator door.

I broached to my parents the notion that cooking school, not a university, was where I belonged, and they told me that while they were not unsympathetic, university, not cooking school, was what they would support. I resisted pointing out that they didn't *have* to support Columbia. I tried arguing with them on the grounds that they, with their active devotion to good food, should find it not simply reasonable but utterly delightful that I wanted to become a chef. They said that as far as they could see, I was already a chef and could improve my skills as much as I needed to at home. Home was for cooking and school was for learning the subjects that would enrich my mental life and provide me with a profession suitable to a young woman from an academic family. When I asked if that wasn't a snobbish argument, serving some notion of who I was supposed to be rather than who I was, my father smiled complacently and said, "Guilty," thus putting an end to the discussion.

The issue was not joined again until a spring evening when we were at dinner. That weekend I'd baby-sat for Jackie while she investigated sharing a summer house in Westhampton, a new location. When I returned on Sunday evening, they were eating in the kitchen. My mail, which included a notice of acceptance from the Culinary Institute, was at my place. I flushed when I saw the envelope. When I had opened and read it, I smiled sadly, put it back in its envelope without speaking and helped myself to some of the cold leftovers on the table.

"Do I gather," my father asked after a while, "that you have applied for admission to this . . . uh . . ."

"School," I said, expressionless. "It's a very good school for cooking. It's called the Culinary Institute of America."

"Indeed," he said. "And have you been accepted?"

"Yes," I said. "I have been accepted. But I can't afford it."

I had been trying to figure out a way, a set of ways, that I could raise the money to attend, but the fee was daunting to someone who had managed to put aside a negligible amount of money. If I'd felt that pleading could get me someplace, I surely would have done it, but I had no hope at all.

"Your mother and I have been talking," my father said to me the following evening. "You know our feelings about paying for—"

"You've told me," I broke in.

"Yes," he said. "Well, we still feel the same way, but it occurred to us . . ."

I looked up, hearing the opening for the first time.

" . . . that there was room for negotiation on the matter."

"Where?" I asked. "What? What do I have to do?"

"Well," he said slowly, "what occurred to us is that while we have the money but don't want to spend it that way, there is another way that we might spend it, without, you might say, compromising our principles. That is, we might spend it to buy something we wanted."

I stared at him uncomprehendingly. He waited. *Something they wanted.* When I finally understood that he was talking about my painting, it was only because there was no other possibility.

He smiled. My mother smiled. They had not been so wrapped up in their work and their social-artistic life as to fail to notice that I was unhappy. Now they were pleased to have found a way to let me do what I wanted to do without compromising their academic principles and while obtaining a painting they would love to own. I was, after all, the only member of the family who possessed an Eleanora Stonepark. They knew from the place in my room to which Jenny had long since been moved that I did not want to look at her.

I could not smile back because my mind, long before it had a reasonable explanation for doing so, refused even to consider letting them have her.

Their smiles faded. I doubt they believed that I would

give up the Culinary Institute before I would part with my picture. But it was occurring to them for the first time that I might not jump at their offer. When I told them days later that even if it meant giving up the Institute, I could not accept, they smiled at each other in sad confirmation: I had always been contrary.

Surely I needed to find a way to be my own person rather than theirs—or, as they would have it, to be contrary. But I don't think contrariness made me cling to my painting. I was beginning to suspect that I would not remain in my parents' home long enough to get a degree. I had no clear idea of what I would do when I left, that is to say, of how close it would be to something I *wanted* to do. I didn't know which of the friends I'd made at school I would keep or whether I would make new ones, nor did I have any assurance that my parents, the fixed point in my life whether I was being my own person or theirs or trying to find some reasonable combination of the two, would remain friendly as I floundered around, looking for a life. But the person in the picture was my assurance that I would find one, and whether I liked her or not, whether or not she made me happy, I needed to keep with me the difficult young woman another difficult woman had named 116th Street Jenny.

JUDITH ROSSNER resides in New York City. She is the author of eight novels, including *Looking for Mr. Goodbar, August,* and *His Little Women.* She is working on a new novel.

GINA BERRIAULT

THE OVERCOAT

The overcoat was black and hung down to his ankles, the sleeves came down to his fingertips, and the weight of it was as much as two overcoats. It was given him by an old girlfriend who wasn't his lover anymore but stayed around just to be his friend. She had chosen it out of a line of Goodwill coats because, since it had already lasted almost a century, it was the most durable and so the right one for his trip to Seattle, a city she imagined as always flooded by cataclysmic rains and cold as an execution dawn.

On the Greyhound bus, the coat overlapped onto the next seat, and only when all the other seats were occupied did a passenger dare to lift it and sit down, women apologetically, men bristling at the coat's invasion of their territory. The coat was formidable. Inside it, he was frail. His friend had filled a paper bag with delicatessen items, hoping to spare him the spectacle of himself at depot counters, hands shaking, coffee spilling, a sight for passengers hungrier for objects of ridicule than for their hamburgers and french fries. So he sat alone in the bus while it cooled under the low ceilings of concrete depots and out in lots under the winter sky, around it piles of wet lumber, cars without tires, shacks, a chained dog, and the cafe's neon sign trembling in the mist.

American Short Fiction, Volume 1, Number 2, Summer 1991

On the last night the bus plowed through roaring rain. Eli sat behind the driver. Panic might take hold of him any moment and he had to be near a door, even the door of this bus crawling along the ocean floor. No one sat beside him, and the voices of the passengers in the dark bus were like the faint chirps of birds about to be swept from their nest. In the glittering tumult of the water beyond the swift arc of the windshield wiper, he was on his way to see his mother and his father, and panic over the sight of them again, and over their sight of him, could wrench him out of his seat and lay him down in the aisle. He pressed his temple against the cold glass and imagined escaping from the bus and from his parents, revived out there in the icy deluge.

For three days he lay in a hotel room in Seattle, unable to face the two he had come so far to see and whom he had not seen in sixteen years, the age he'd been when he'd seen them last. They were already old when he was a kid, at least in his eyes, and now they seemed beyond age. The room was cold and clammy, but he could have sworn a steam radiator was on, hissing and sputtering. Then he figured an old man was sitting in a corner, watching over him, sniffling and sadly whistling. Until he took the noise by surprise and caught it coming from his own nose and mouth. Lying under an army blanket and his overcoat, he wished he had waited until summer. But all waiting time was dangerous. Winter was the best time for him anyway. The overcoat was an impenetrable cover for his wasted body, for his arms lacerated by needles, scar on scar, and decorated with prison tattoos. Even if it were summer he'd wear the coat. The sun would have to get even fiercer than in that story he'd read when he was a kid, about the sun and the wind betting each other which of them could take off the man's coat, and the sun won. Then he'd take off his coat, he'd even take off his shirt, and his parents would see who had been hiding inside. They'd see Eli under the sun.

With his face bundled up in a yellow plaid muffler he'd found on the floor of the bus, he went by ferry and by more buses way out to the edge of this watery state, avoiding his mother by first visiting his father. Clumping down to the fishing boats riding on the glacial gray sea, he was thrown off course by panic, by the presence of his father in one of those boats, and he zigzagged around the little town like an immense black beetle blown across the ocean from its own fantastic region.

On the deck of his father's boat he was instantly dizzied by the lift and fall and the jolting against the wharf, and he held to the rail of the steep steps down to the cabin, afraid he was going to be thrown onto his father, entangling them in another awful mishap.

"Eli, Eli here," he said.

"Eli?"

"That's me," he said.

Granite, his father had turned to granite. The man sitting on the bunk was gray, face gray, skimpy hair gray, the red net of broken capillaries become black flecks, and he didn't move. The years had chiseled him down to nowhere near the size he'd been.

"Got arthritis in my knees," his father said. The throat, could it catch arthritis too? His voice was the high-pitched whisper of a woman struggling with a man, it was Eli's mother's voice, changed places. "Got it from the damn wet, took too many falls."

The Indian woman, beside him, shook tobacco from a pouch, rolled the cigarette, licked it closed, and never looked up. She must be thinking Eli was a visitor who came by every day.

"You want to sit?" his father said.

Eli sat on the bunk opposite them and his father poured him a glass of port. The storm had roughed things up, his father said, and Eli told them about the bus battling the rain all night. The woman asked Eli if anything was stolen from his boat while he was away, and he humored her, he said a watch was stolen, and his shortwave radio.

"That's a big overcoat you got there," his father said. "You prosperous?"

"Oh yes!" he said. "I'm so prosperous I got a lot of parasites living off me."

The Indian woman laughed. "They relatives of yours?"

"Anything living off you is a relative," he said.

The woman pushed herself up in stages, her weight giving her a hard time as if it were a penalty. She wore two pairs of thick socks, the holes in the top pair showing the socks underneath. Her breasts hung to her waist though she had no waist, but when she lifted her arms to light a hanging kerosene lamp, he saw how gracefully she did it, her hands acting like a pretty girl's. He might fall for her himself if he were sixteen.

They did not offer him dinner. They must have eaten theirs already.

"I've got no place to sleep," he said.

They let him sleep on the bunk. They slept aft, far back in a dark space. He lay in his overcoat, drawing his legs up close against his stomach, and his feet in socks got warm. Then he thought he was a boy again, home again in the house in Seattle, under covers in his own bed while his parents drank the night away, unprotected from them but protected by them from the dreadful world they warned him about, out there.

At dawn he was waked by his shivering body. Out on the pier, the salt cold wind stiffened him, almost blinding him, so that he wound up a few times at the pier's edges. When you look back, he'd heard, you're turned to salt, and that's what was happening to him. If he fell into the sea he'd disappear faster than fate intended.

For two days he wandered around Seattle, avoiding his mother. Now that he was near to her, he wanted to go on by. He had betrayed her. *Tell me about your parents, Eli.*

Strangers, creepy parole officers and boyface psychiatrists in leather jackets and women social workers whose thighs he had hoped to open with the shining need for love in his eyes, each of them jiving with him like a cellmate, and all of them urging him to tell about a woman they could never know. He had betrayed her, he had blamed her for Eli, and blamed the old man on the rocking boat. Those strangers had cut out his heart with their prying, and remorse had always rushed in to fill up the empty space where his heart had been.

They told him at the desk that his mother was ambulatory and could be anywhere. His father had called this a rest home, and he wondered why they were resting in here when all that rest was just ahead for them. The women in the rows of narrow beds he passed, and the women in their chairs between the beds, hadn't much left of womanness in them, but their power over him was intact. He went along before their pale faces staring out at the last puzzling details of the world, himself a detail, a cowering man in a long black overcoat who might be old enough to be their dead father.

There she was, far down a corridor and out, and he followed her into a paved yard, walled in by brick and concrete. She put her hand to the wall to aid herself in open space, reached the bench, and sat down, and her profile assured him that he wasn't mistaken.

"Mother, it's Eli," he said.

She raised her eyes, and one eye was shrewd and the other as purely open as a child's, the blue almost as blue as ever.

"Eli," he said. "Can I sit down?"

"Room enough for everybody."

He sat, and she paid him no attention. From a pocket of her sweater she took a scrap of comb and began to comb her hair. The comb went cautiously through the limp hair still feisty red. She was twenty years younger than his father but keeping up with him on the way out, and their son Eli, their only child, was keeping up with them both.

"We had ourselves an earthquake," she said. "Bricks fell down. We thought the whole damn place was coming down. Did you feel it?"

"I wasn't here," he said.

"Were you scared?"

"I wasn't here."

"I bet you were scared."

"I died in it," he said.

If she wanted his company in her earthquake it was no trouble to oblige. It made no difference, afterwards, when or where you died, and it was easier to tell her he was already dead than tell her he was going to be soon, even before he could get up from this bench.

"Poor boy," she said. But slowly, still combing her hair, she turned her head to take another look at him, this man who had sat down beside her to belittle her with his lies. "You never died," she said. "You're alive as me."

Off in a corner and facing the wall, he pulled up the overcoat to cover his head and in that dark tent wept over them, over her and himself and his father, all so baffled by what was going on and what had gone on in their lives and what was to go on. Grief for the three of them filled up the overcoat's empty space, leaving no room to spare. ☙

GINA BERRIAULT lives in California. She has written short stories, novels, articles, and screenplays, and has taught at the University of Iowa's Writers Workshop and in the School of Humanities, San Francisco State University. Ms. Berriault has been awarded fellowships by the Guggenheim Foundation, the National Endowment for the Arts, the Radcliffe Institute for Independent Studies, and the Ingram Merrill Foundation. Her most recent publications are *The Infinite Passion of Expectation,* a collection of stories, and *The Lights of Earth,* a novel.

NAGUIB MAHFOUZ

BLESSED NIGHT

translated by Denys Johnson-Davies

It was nothing but a single room in the unpretentious Nouri Alley, off Clot Bey Street. In the middle of the room was the bar and the shelf embellished with bottles. It was called The Flower and was passionately patronized by old men addicted to drink. Its barman was advanced in years, excessively quiet, a man who inspired silence and yet effused a cordial friendliness. Unlike other taverns, The Flower dozed in a delightful tranquility. The regulars would converse inwardly, with glances rather than words. On the night that was blessed, the barman departed from his traditional silence.

"Yesterday," he said, "I dreamed that a gift would be presented to a man of good fortune. . . ."

Safwan's heart broke into a song with gentle lute accompaniment, while alcoholic waves flowed through him like electricity as he congratulated himself with the words "O blessed, blessed night!" He left the bar, reeling drunk, and plunged into the sublime night under an autumn sky that was not without a twinkling of stars. He made his way toward Nuzha Street, cutting across the square, glowing with an intoxication unadulterated by the least sensation of drowsiness. The street was humbled under the veil of

American Short Fiction, Volume 1, Number 2, Summer 1991

darkness, except for the light from the regularly spaced streetlamps, the shops having closed their doors and given themselves up to sleep. He stood in front of his house: the fourth on the right, Number 42, a single-storied house fronted by an old courtyard of whose garden nothing remained but a solitary towering date palm. Astonished at the dense darkness that surrounded the house, he wondered why his wife had not as usual turned on the light by the front door. It seemed that the house was manifesting itself in a new, gloomily forlorn shape and that it exuded a smell like that of old age. Raising his voice, he called out. "Hey there!"

From behind the fence there rose before his eyes the form of a man, who coughed and inquired, "Who are you? What do you want?"

Safwan was startled at the presence of this stranger and asked sharply, "And who are you? What's brought you to my house?"

"Your house?" said the man in a hoarse, angry voice.

"Who are you?"

"I am the guardian for religious endowment properties."

"But this is my house."

"This house has been deserted for ages," the man scoffed. "People avoid it because it's rumored to be haunted by spirits."

Safwan decided he must have lost his way, and hurried back toward the square. He gave it a long comprehensive look, then raised his head to the street sign and read out loud, "Nuzha." So again he entered the street and counted off the houses until he arrived at the fourth. There he stood in a state of bewilderment, almost of panic: he could find neither his own house nor the haunted one. Instead he saw an empty space, a stretch of wasteland lying between the other houses. "Is it my house that I've lost or my mind?" he wondered.

He saw a policeman approaching, examining the locks of the shops. He stood in his path and pointed toward the empty wasteland. "What do you see there?"

The policeman stared at him suspiciously and muttered, "As you can see, it's a piece of wasteland where they sometimes set up funeral pavilions."

"That's just where I should have found my house," said Safwan. "I left it there with my wife inside it in the pink of health only this afternoon, so when could it have been pulled down and all the rubble cleared away?"

The policeman concealed an involuntary smile behind a stern official glare and said brusquely, "Ask that deadly poison in your stomach!"

"You are addressing a former general manager," said Safwan haughtily. At this the policeman grasped him by the arm and led him off. "Drunk and disorderly in the public highway!"

He took Safwan to the Daher police station, a short distance away, where he was brought before the officer on a charge of being drunk and disorderly. The officer took pity on him, however, because of his age and his respectable appearance. "Your identity card?"

Safwan produced it and said, "I'm quite in my right mind, it's just that there's no trace of my house."

"Well, now there's a new type of theft!" said the officer, laughing. "I really don't believe it!"

"But I'm speaking the truth," said Safwan in alarm.

"The truth's being unfairly treated, but I'll be lenient in deference to your age." Then he said to the policeman, "Take him to Number 42 Nuzha Street."

Accompanied by the policeman, Safwan finally found himself in front of his house as he knew it. Despite his drunken state he was overcome with confusion. He opened the outer door, crossed the courtyard, and put on the light at the entrance, where he was immediately taken aback, for he found himself in an entrance he had never before set eyes on. There was absolutely no connection between it and the entrance of the house in which he had lived for about half a century, and whose furniture and walls were all in a state of decay. He decided to retreat before his mistake was revealed, so he darted into the street, where he stood scrutinizing the house from the outside. It was his house all right, from the point of view of its features and site, and he had opened the door with his own key, no doubt about it. What, then, had changed the inside? He had seen a small chandelier, and the walls had been papered. There was also a new carpet. In a way it was his house, and in another way it was not. And what about his wife, Sadriyya? "I've been drinking for half a century," he said aloud, "so what is it about this blessed night?"

He imagined his seven married daughters looking at him with tearful eyes. He determined, though, to solve the problem by himself, without recourse to the authorities—which would certainly mean exposing himself to the wrath of the law. Going up to the fence, he began clapping his hands, at which the front door was opened by someone whose features he could not make out. A woman's voice could be heard asking, "What's keeping you outside?"

It seemed, though he could not be certain, that it was the voice of a stranger. "Whose house is this, please?" he inquired.

"Are you that drunk? It's just too much!"

"I'm Safwan," he said cautiously.

"Come in or you'll wake the people sleeping."

"Are you Sadriyya?"

"Heaven help us! There's someone waiting for you inside."

"At this hour?"

"He's been waiting since ten."

"Waiting for me?"

She mumbled loudly in exasperation, and he inquired again, "Are you Sadriyya?"

Her patience at an end, she shouted, "Heaven help us!"

He advanced, at first stealthily, then without caring, and found himself in the new entrance. He saw that the door of the sitting room was open, with the lights brightly illuminating the interior. As for the woman, she had disappeared. He entered the sitting room, which revealed itself to him in a new garb, as the entrance had. Where had the old room with its ancient furniture gone to? Walls recently painted and a large chandelier from which Spanish-style lamps hung, a blue carpet, a spacious sofa, and armchairs: it was a splendid room. In the foreground sat a man he had not seen before: thin, of a dark brown complexion, with a nose reminding one of a parrot's beak, and a certain impetuosity in the eyes. He was wearing a black suit, although autumn was only just coming in. The man addressed him irritably. "How late you are for our appointment!"

Safwan was both taken aback and angry. "What appointment? Who are you?"

"That's just what I expected—you'd forgotten!" the man exclaimed. "It's the same old complaint repeated every single day, whether it's the truth or not. It's no use, it's out of the question. . . ."

"What is this raving nonsense?" Safwan shouted in exasperation.

Restraining himself, the man said, "I know you're a man who enjoys his drink and sometimes overdoes it."

"You're speaking to me as though you were in charge of me, while I don't even know you. I'm amazed you should impose your presence on a house in the absence of its owner."

He gave a chilly smile. "Its owner?"

"As though you doubt it!" Safwan said vehemently. "I see I'll have to call the police."

"So they can arrest you for being drunk and disorderly—and for fraud?"

"Shut up—you insolent impostor!"

The man struck one palm against the other and said, "You're pretending not to know who I am so as to escape from your commitments. It's out of the question . . ."

"I don't know you and I don't know what you're talking about."

"Really? Are you alleging you forgot and are therefore innocent? Didn't you agree to sell your house and wife, and fix tonight for completing the final formalities?"

Safwan, in a daze, exclaimed, "What a lying devil you are!"

"As usual. You're all the same—shame on you!" said the other, with a shrug of the shoulders.

"You're clearly mad."

"I have the proof and witnesses."

"I've never heard of anyone having done such a thing before."

"But it happens every moment. You're putting on a good act, even though you're drunk."

In extreme agitation, Safwan said, "I demand you leave at once."

"No, let's conclude the incompleted formalities," said the other in a voice full of confidence.

He got up and went toward the closed door that led to the interior of the house. He rapped on it, then returned to his seat. Immediately there entered a short man with a pug nose and prominent forehead, carrying under his arm a file stuffed with papers. He bowed in greeting and sat down. Safwan directed a venomous glare at him and exclaimed, "Since when has my house become a shelter for the homeless?"

The first man, introducing the person who had just entered, said, "The lawyer."

At which Safwan asked him brusquely, "And who gave you permission to enter my house?"

"You're in a bad way," said the lawyer, smiling, "but may God forgive you. What are you so angry about?"

"What insolence!"

Without paying any attention to what Safwan had said, the lawyer went on. "The deal is undoubtedly to your advantage."

"What deal?" asked Safwan in bewilderment.

"You know exactly what I mean, and I would like to tell you that it's useless your thinking of going back on it now. The law is on our side, and common sense too. Let me ask you: Do you consider this house to be really yours?"

For the first time Safwan felt at a loss. "Yes and no," he said.

"Was it in this condition when you left it?"

"Not at all."

"Then it's another house?"

"Yet it's the same site, number, and street."

"Ah, those are fortuitous incidentals that don't affect the essential fact—and there's something else."

He got up, rapped on the door, and returned to his seat. All at once a beautiful middle-aged woman, well dressed and with a mournful mien, entered and seated herself alongside the first man. The lawyer resumed his questioning. "Do you recognize in this lady your wife?"

It seemed to Safwan that she did possess a certain similarity, but he could not stop himself from saying, "Not at all."

"Fine—the house is neither your house, nor the lady your wife. Thus nothing remains but for you to sign the final agreement and then you can be off. . . ."

"Off! Where to?"

"My dear sir, don't be stubborn. The deal is wholly to your advantage, and you know it."

The telephone rang, although it was very late at night. The caller was the barman. Safwan was astonished that the man should be telephoning him for the first time in his life. "Safwan Bey," he said, "Sign without delay."

"But do you know. . . ."

"Sign. It's the chance of a lifetime."

The receiver was replaced at the other end. Safwan considered the short conversation and found himself relaxing. In a second his state of mind changed utterly, his face took on a cheerful expression, and a sensation of calm spread throughout his body. The feeling of tension left him, and he signed. When he had done so, the lawyer handed him a small but somewhat heavy suitcase and said, "May the Almighty bless your comings and goings. In this suitcase is all that a happy man needs in this world."

The first man clapped, and there entered an extremely portly man, with a wide smile and a charming manner. Introducing him to Safwan, the lawyer said, "This is a trustworthy man and an expert at his work. He will take you to your new abode. It is truly a profitable deal."

The portly man made his way outside, and Safwan followed him, quiet and calm, his hand gripping the handle of the suitcase. The man walked ahead of him into the night, and Safwan followed. Affected by the fresh air, he staggered and realized that he had not recovered from the intoxication of the blessed night. The man quickened his pace, and the distance between them grew, so Safwan in turn, despite his drunken state, walked faster, his gaze directed toward the specter of the other man, while wondering how it was that he combined such agility with portliness. "Take it easy, sir!" Safwan called out to him.

But it was as though he had spurred the man on to greater speed, for he broke into strides so rapid that Safwan was forced to hurl himself forward for fear he would lose him, and thus lose his last hope. Frightened he would be incapable of keeping up the pace, he once again called out to the man. "Take it easy or I'll get lost!"

At this the other, unconcerned about Safwan, began to run. Safwan, in terror, raced ahead, heedless of the consequences. This caused him great distress, but all to no avail, for the man plunged into the darkness and disappeared from sight. Safwan was frightened the man would arrive ahead of him at Yanabi Square, where various roads split up, and he would not know which one the man had taken. He therefore began running as fast as possible, determined to catch up.

His efforts paid off, for once again he caught a glimpse of the specter of the man at the crossroads. He saw him darting forward toward the fields, ignoring the branch roads that turned off to the eastern and western parts of the city. Safwan hurried along behind him and continued running without stopping, and without the least feeling of weakness. His nostrils were filled with delightful aromas that stirred up all kinds of sensations he had never before properly experienced and enjoyed.

When the two of them were alone in the vast void of earth and sky, the portly man gradually began to slow down until he had reverted to a mere brisk trot, then to a walk. Finally he stopped, and Safwan caught up with him and also came to a breathless stop. He looked around at the all-pervading darkness, with the glittering lights of faint stars. "Where's the new abode?" he asked.

The man maintained his silence. At the same time, Safwan began to feel the incursion of a new weight bearing down upon his shoulders and his whole body. The weight grew heavier and heavier and then rose upward to his head. It seemed to him that his feet would plunge deep into the ground. The pressure became so great that he could no longer bear it and, with a sudden spontaneous burst of energy, he took off his shoes. Then, the pressure working its way upwards, he stripped himself of his jacket and trousers and flung them to the ground. This made no real difference, so he rid himself of his underclothes, heedless of the dampness of autumn. He was ablaze with pain and, groaning, he abandoned the suitcase on the ground. At that moment it seemed to him that he had regained his balance, that he was capable of taking the few steps that still remained. He waited for his companion to do something, but the man was sunk in silence. Safwan wanted to converse with him, but talk was impossible, and the overwhelming silence slipped through the pores of his skin to his very heart. It seemed that in a little while he would be hearing the conversation that was passing between the stars. ☙

NAGUIB MAHFOUZ was born in Cairo in 1911 and began writing when he was seventeen. He has more than thirty novels to his credit, ranging from his earliest historical romances to his most recent experimental novels. "Blessed Night" is included in his first collection of stories to appear in English, entitled *The Time and the Place and Other Stories,* which will be published by Doubleday in June. In 1988, Mr. Mahfouz was awarded the Nobel Prize for Literature. He lives in the Cairo suburb of Agouza with his wife and two daughters.

DENYS JOHNSON-DAVIES was born in Vancouver in 1922, began studying Arabic at the School of Oriental Studies, London University, in 1937, and later took a degree at Cambridge. Among his published translations are *The Mountain of Green Tea* by Yehya Taher Abdullah and *Music of Human Flesh* by Mahmoud Darwish.

WILLIAM HUMPHREY

THE APPLE OF DISCORD

I

An old apple, a rotten apple, the last one from the bottom of the barrel, shriveled, mottled: that was what his face had come to look like. It was moldy with whiskers now that shaving had become awkward for him, and he sullen and resentful and careless of his appearance. To do it at all after his accident he had had to buy this electric razor. With that clumsy right hand of his he would have peeled himself using a blade. But today was the Big Day, weeks in preparation. Today he was to give away the last of his daughters, and he must put on the best face he could for the occasion, and show that he could be gracious in defeat.

Today's would be the third wedding in the house in as many years. Generations of Bennetts had been married under this roof in apple-blossom time, the family tradition. Now after this one there would be no more—never.

Of his three girls the first to leave home was Ellen, the oldest. He had opposed her marriage. He opposed it not only because her intended was not what he wasn't, an orchardman, but also because he was what he was, a preacher. He let his prospective son-in-law know just where he and his boss stood with him. Who was it who sent His

American Short Fiction, Volume 1, Number 2, Summer 1991

sun and His rain to swell and sweeten and color the fruit on the Bennett trees? He who sent His frost and His hail and His drought and His mold and His bugs to blight and destroy it. *As surely as God made little green apples?* But God didn't make them—*he* did, and God put all His obstacles in his way. He thought of himself with his trees as like one of those welfare mothers abandoned by the father of her children and struggling to raise them on her own. His charges numbered somewhere around ten thousand.

He told the preacher the old story of Farmer Brown. How, after being wiped out repeatedly by all the afflictions of Job, Farmer Brown raised his eyes to heaven and asked, "Dear God, what have I done to deserve this?" "Farmer Brown," said God, "you don't have to 'do' anything. There's just something about you that pisses me off." He himself was surely one of God's chosen, for those whom He loved He scourged and chastened. He was a Bennett, one of the spawn of the original apple-vendor. God had borne a grudge against that forbidden fruit ever since Eve.

He paused in his shaving for a moment to think about that ancestress of his. The first woman! The original! What a woman that one must have been! What a prize! In the fall of the mother of them all, all would fall. A temptation . . . Furs? Jewels? The lure of a tropical cruise? There where the timeless fashions were the design of the Master and any ornament a detraction from the female form divine? A vacation from Paradise? Another, more attractive man? There was no other man, nor could one ever again be so attractive. Hers was the mold, and castings from it could only approximate the original. Something to tempt her to transgress against her Maker's one prohibition . . .

Something good to eat. Something never before eaten. And so she could not know whether it was good to eat or not. But she could tell just by looking. A thing mouth-watering enough to entice her to disobey the command of the Almighty and risk bringing down upon herself His wrath. There in that Garden of Earthly Delights were all the sweets: pomegranates and peaches and plums, figs, grapes, mangoes—everything to be found in your local supermarket flown in from all over the world, only tree-ripened: cactus pears, pineapples, bananas. But to tempt the original sinner to commit the original sin Satan picked from among the produce the one irresistible one. None of your kiwis nor your passion fruit. And Adam, well aware of what he was up to, and what he was incurring, not even chewing but trying to swallow it down whole. It was for having eaten of the fruit of the tree of the knowledge of good and evil that the first couple were expelled from their garden, before they could find their way to the tree of life everlasting. Well, life everlasting they may have lost by eating that apple, but what fruit, one a day, kept the doctor away? Not prunes, friend.

And now another of God's pranks upon His servant Seth: a preacher for a son-in-law.

Ellen revealed a willfulness that he would sooner have expected of either of her sisters. That lifelong docility and dutifulness of hers seemed to have been building up like water behind a dam. It now burst. It almost made him change his mind about her and press his opposition to the marriage harder. Maybe she had in her more of the grit of which farmwives were made than he had given her credit for. But orchardmen were getting scarce hereabouts. It was unrealistic of him to hope any longer to find ones for all three girls. Let Ellen have her preacher. The blessing he gave her was grudging, but he gave it. Write her off as the wild card in the deck; he had two more to deal.

He lowered the razor and peered at his face in the mirror, searching in vain for a likeness between himself and his offspring. Those stepdaughters of Eve, his daughters, they none of them cared for apples. Bennetts—and they didn't care for apples! Doris, the "in-between one," as she called herself, wouldn't touch one. Said she knew too well what work and worry had gone into it. Said that for her the sight of her poor mother, her old knees ruined long ago from kneeling to sort them, put a worm in each and every one. As for him, well, never mind how old he was but he was old—people told him so to his face: "I can't blame you for selling out. You've got nobody to leave the place to and you'll soon be too old to work it yourself anymore." He had attained his age by eating apples enough each day to keep three doctors away.

Who were those girls of his to say they didn't want to be apple farmers? Neither had he "wanted" to be one. He was *born* one. He did not choose, he was chosen. He had not asked to be left-handed, green-eyed, red-headed either, but so he was. He had cut his teeth on apples. That was what it was to be a Bennett!

He had put all three through college. He was not one of those who thought that higher education was not for women; on the contrary, he thought it was for women only—men were meant for practical affairs. How had he paid for their tuition? With Macintoshes, Cortlands, Macouns, Red Delicious, Greenings: so many crates per credit-hour. The fruit of knowledge. Apples for the teacher. The best schooling. Vassar College! The mistake of his life. How you gonna keep 'em down on the farm after they've seen Poughkeepsie?

Why had the farmboys he exposed them to all been so backward? No boldness, no spunk in any of them. To get that dowry of ten thousand trees, bridal-like with blossoms in the spring, aglow with fruit in the fall, he would have seduced one of the farmer's daughters, any one, hoping that she got caught and he be marched to the altar by her old man with a shotgun at his back, chortling to himself all the way up the aisle.

Certainly none of those boys could have held back out

of fear that the girl's father found him unacceptable on closer inspection. He was prepared to overlook shortcomings. He encouraged them. He bucked them up when their hopes flagged. Certain shortcomings he was looking for in his sons-in-law. It was doubly frustrating because the very backwardness—sometimes the none-too-brightness—that kept them from putting themselves forward was the attribute he sought. Broad backs and brawny arms were what they were to furnish—his girls would supply the brains. He wanted his daughters to wear the pants in their families. He wanted them to twist their husbands around their little fingers.

His stock of daughters dwindling, he opposed Doris's marriage more vigorously by far than he had opposed Ellen's. Another nonfarmer. An undertaker—"mortician," he preferred to be called. Somebody had to do it, of course. Nothing more essential. But what more thankless a job was there? How could she sleep at night knowing what thing lay on that marble slab in the basement workshop? How could she tolerate the touch of those hands of his, knowing what they had been busy at earlier in the day? How could you raise your children in a charnel house, and how did other children look on yours? How could you bear to be always in the hush of mourning among grieving survivors dressed in black? Why not a doctor instead, somebody whose business it was to keep people alive? Or better still, an apple farmer, one whose job it was to keep the doctor away.

So with two down and only one to go, he now had for sons-in-law one to put him under and another to get him a pass to that nursing home in the sky where you play bingo in eternity. The pair of them often teamed up on the same case. This thought would in time put into his mind a scheme. A way of ensuring that his third and last son-in-law be the orchardman he wanted. More specifically, Pete

Jeffers, a man like himself, with cider, hard cider, in his veins.

One man's misfortune is another man's fortune. He had sometimes been the beneficiary of that one-sided exchange, though always mindful that it might just as easily have been the other way round. Apple farming had its rewards but it was a risky business. It could drive you to desperation. It could drive you crazy.

Some years ago a neighbor of his caught a woman in his orchard threshing one of the trees. He was a worried man. Crops had been poor for years and this one promised to be no better. He was deeply in debt. The chronic shortage of pickers had forced him into the pick-your-own business, something no farmer liked because in picking the apples inexperienced pickers broke off the buds of many of next year's apples. Now the man went berserk. He grabbed the woman's stick from her and threshed her with it. She died from a blow to her head. He spent the rest of his life in the state asylum for the criminally insane. The farm his family was forced to sell became part of Seth Bennett's.

Of all the natural enemies of orchardmen the two most dreaded were a late spring frost when the trees were in blossom and a summer hailstorm when the fruit was on them. You could spray against insects and fungus, you could poison the mice that girdled the trees and the woodchucks that burrowed beneath their roots, shoot the deer, but against frost and hail you were helpless. If the fruit was not destroyed by the hail, it was pocked, unappetizing-looking, unmarketable except to the baby-food processors, for a portion of the price it would have fetched. That insurance against it was available was a bad joke; nobody could afford the premium.

After losing his wife to cancer, then being wiped out by hail two years in a row, Seth Bennett's neighbor Tom Jeffers went out in his ruined orchard and put a bullet in his heart. He left his only child Pete to sell out to developers and pay off his debts. Pete had lived at home, his father's partner.

Seth Bennett felt beholden to Pete Jeffers as a combat veteran might have felt toward the orphan of a buddy who had taken the bullets meant for them both. For although their two farms were little more than a mile apart, such was the capriciousness of hail that his had been spared both times by the storms that struck Tom Jeffers' twice.

Of late, on nights when the trees had to be sprayed, it was Janet, home from school now, who drove the tractor that pulled him on the sprayer. She would not allow her mother, with those knees of hers, to spend the night out in the chill and the damp.

Now that the two older girls were gone from home their rooms were unused. Pete Jeffers was homeless. Pete knew apples. Molly was old. So, for that matter, was he. He could use a helper, an experienced hand. Pete was a fine fellow. Quiet, serious-minded, with a farmer's patience and tenacity. Pete was unmarried. He was just three years older than Janet.

To the sign on the road that read, "Garden of Eden Orchards. Pick Your Own. Seth Bennett, Prop." was now added, "Peter Jeffers, Manager."

"I want you to think of us as your family, Pete," he said.

Including Janet, he added to himself. But not as your sister.

What a workhorse the man turned out to be! Never still. Busy every minute of the day. Handy at everything, not just at the daily farm duties. Fixed, patched, mended, repaired, painted, cleaned, straightened—things needing doing for years. Even on Sundays. So eager to be doing he had no time for talk at table, was up and out while still chewing. This during the off-season. The time came to gear up for the year's crop. What that young fellow didn't know about apple farming wasn't worth knowing. Born to it, in it all his life, had it in his blood. What a treasure he would be when he took over the place!

Trouble was, you couldn't get him to slow down long enough to spend any time with Janet. Was there another woman in his life? That would be a sorry repayment for the hospitality he had been shown as a homeless orphan! But no, there could be no other woman: he never left the place, never took a minute off much less a night out. His would-be father-in-law began to wonder whether Pete was not one of those born bachelors, living only to work. He seemed to have no pleasures, no personal life. Busying himself to keep his mind off his parents, said Seth to himself, and waited for Pete to come out of his mourning and take notice of the world around him.

Meanwhile, to hasten that process he threw the two of them together whenever possible—and groaned inwardly at Pete's backwardness as he spied on them. "Molly's knees are bad this evening," he would say, giving her a look, after dinner. "Pete, be a good boy and dry the dishes for Janet." Pete did, and that was all he did: dry dishes. The evening still young, Seth would excuse himself, and Molly, for bed, and he was scarcely out of his recliner before Pete was out of his armchair, saying good night to all. Her father bought Janet a car, her first, and Pete taught her to drive. Seated that close, on back country roads, lovers' lanes . . . Janet passed her license test on her first try.

"Pete," he said, "let's you and me have a talk. Father to son. I think of you as my adopted son. Who knows?—maybe one day soon we will be closer than that. My hope is that we will.

"As you know, I've got no son of my own to leave the farm to. What I have got is one daughter still unmarried. As far as I'm concerned, she's yours if you want her."

"But she doesn't like me."

"What are you saying! Of course she likes you."

"I don't mean she *dislikes* me. But she doesn't *like* me."

"Don't I know her? Do I know this old palm of mine? My own daughter? I know her better than she knows herself. I tell you she likes you."

"Then she certainly doesn't show it."

"You don't understand women. They're supposed to play hard to get. Would you want one who threw herself at you? You appreciate them more if you have to overcome some resistance. They're like horses: they have to be broken. They shy from you at first and dash all over the lot, but their curiosity about you is aroused and in time they come to your whistle and nuzzle you as you slip the halter over their heads. They'll buck and throw you when you first try to mount them but they accept your weight after a while. Well, I took that a little further than I meant to, but my point is made. Keep after her, boy. Faint heart never won fair lady. Maybe you don't like her enough?"

"Oh, yes, I do. She's attractive. She's bright. Educated. Has an agreeable disposition. Everything a man could want in a wife."

"And with her comes the farm. Ten thousand trees! Three hundred and twenty acres! A kingdom all your own! And more than that: Molly and me. You have to think of that, too. Sometimes, you know, in-laws don't get along so well—especially when they live under the same roof. In fact, there are people who, although they want their daughter to marry, resent the man who takes her from them. It's contrary, still, that's human nature for you. But we would welcome you into the family. You have my blessing. And I can speak for Molly, too. Now it's up to you, son. She's just waiting for you to make known your intentions. Take my word."

One variety of apple, just one, the Cortland, consistently twinned: two stems from a common bud, the identical fruit hanging cheek by cheek. He and his Janet were a pair of Cortlands. Neither of them could think a thought without the other knowing it. She would understand what was expected of her now. Her sisters having married to their father's disappointment, it was up to her to put things right. Child of her parents' old age, plainly the last, she had been petted by all the family, given her own way in everything. She was deeply in their debt. The time had come for her to discharge that debt.

"Well, Janet, I suppose you'll be thinking of getting married before long now." Her sister Doris's wedding was barely over before he said that to her.

"I'm not in any hurry," she said.

But he was. He was still a long way from the finish line, but his face as he shaved every morning (this was before he broke his left arm) told him that he was in the home stretch. Janet must be spurred.

The tombstone-cutter he went to was the son, maybe the grandson, of the one with whom he had last dealt. That occasion was the burial of his mother. The Bennetts were a long-lived clan. In their old family graveyard on the farm lay many who had lasted into their nineties. And that was before the miracles of modern medicine.

The stonecutter was putting the finishing touches to a job; be right with him. He wore goggles, and over his nose and mouth a mask. Through a rubber stencil glued to the face of the stone, he was carving the last digit in the date of some person's death. He did it not with a hammer and chisel but with a jet of fine metal pellets propelled by an airbrush like the charge of a shotgun. To protect himself from their rebound he wore a blacksmith's leather apron. He now finished his job, pushed up his goggles and pulled down his mask, peeled off the stencil, ran his forefinger over the engraving, and gave a nod of approval.

When he learned that the stone his customer wanted to

order was one for himself and his wife the mason commended his good sense and his consideration for his heirs. It was so right and yet so rare. Knowing his true motive, and protected by his heritage of longevity, Seth enjoyed the man's misplaced admiration for what he took to be his foresight.

"I can't think of a more important decision for people to make for themselves, nor one more personal. Yet most of them can't bring themselves to do it. And that's foolish because, let's face it, the time is coming—which of us knows when?—and the sensible thing is to do it while you can, the way *you* want it done, not leave it to your survivors. I've seen them here almost come to blows over what Mom or Pop would have liked. Children all have different notions one from another about their parents, and nothing brings it out like that last decision. In the end, with the best intentions in the world, they may choose something you wouldn't think suitable for you at all, and whatever it is you're the one who's going to have to live with it, so to speak, 'in perpetuity,' as we say."

They were now outdoors where the firm's wares were displayed, a selection of stones, clean-faced, innocent of inscription, like an orphanage standing at inspection for a choice of adoption and the bestowal of a name.

"What I want is simple," he said. "A single stone for my wife and myself. Here. I've written it down. It's to read, 'Seth. Molly.' Underneath each name the years of birth and death. Then this epitaph: 'Comfort me with apples. . . .'"

"With, of course, the family name. I mention that because we charge by the letter."

"That won't be necessary. Anyone who sees it will know."

"Well. I'll put your information, your vital statistics, as we say, on file, and the stone will be carved and put in place after the burial of whichever of you survives the other."

"I'd like to have it in place by this time next week."

"While both of you are still alive?"

"That's why I'm buying it now."

"Burial is difficult when the stone is already in place. The backhoe disturbs it."

"In this case there will be little disturbance. We're going to be cremated."

They would have been even if the modern sanitary code had not prescribed it in cases of burial in private family graveyards. He had no intention of spending his last night above ground on that marble slab in his son-in-law's basement.

"Is it to go in the Protestant cemetery or the Catholic?"

"Neither."

The family graveyard lay out of sight of the house at a distance of a hundred yards. In it were buried three generations of Bennetts—with space remaining for several more, descendants to come of that son-in-law, the orchardman, whom he was bent on having. All his life long he had laid flowers on those graves, had mowed and weeded and raked among them, had straightened their headstones after the heavings of the frost. He had lived to an age that made even those of his dead whom he remembered remote in time from him. Of the others he had forgotten just what the kinship to him of many of them was. But the knowledge was comforting that all were his, Bennetts by birth or grafted onto the stock, tenants of his domain. Comforting, too, was the old-fashioned quaintness of their headstones: weatherworn, mossy tablets of white marble, some with inscriptions so effaced by time and the elements as to be nearly indecipherable, others with their stilted epitaphs and archaic spelling, they made death seem like something that used to happen to people.

The transaction was concluded with, "Mr. Bennett, sir, we appreciate your patronage, and," pointing with his pencil first to the blank space following the year of Seth's birth, and the dash following that, then to Molly's, "may it be a long time before I'm called on to fill in those."

He could not resist saying, "Hold on, young fellow. When that time comes you may not be here yourself."

"How well I know! But if I'm not, somebody will be."

The mason and his crew with their crane and backhoe arrived on the worksite after Janet went off to her job in the morning and were finished and gone by the time she got home in the evening. Thus she never knew the stone was there until he showed it to her.

He was pleased with his production. The setting: soil sacred to her family, its shrine, its collective crypt. The cast: all her ancestors, born here, buried here, in unbroken line of succession, inheritance. She could not but feel their eloquent silence, their call, their claim on her. Each marble marker was the tablet of the law, proclaiming her identity, her duty. And now this latest one, her parents', with its impending dates, its Biblical injunction, passed on the torch to her. From out of the corner of his eye he slyly studied its effect.

It was quick in coming.

"Oh, Father!" she cried, and burst into tears.

She had never called him "Father" before, always "Papa," and the unaccustomed name distanced him from himself, made him feel as though he was being spoken of in the third person, posthumously.

She flung herself, sobbing, into his arms.

Shaken, shamed, he said, patting her back, "Now, now. I'm not under there yet," although he could almost feel the weight upon him of that granite block, which stared at him over her heaving shoulder. It now seemed to him the worst of bad jokes at his own expense, and there it would sit to mock him with that blank space waiting to be filled in. "It's just the sensible thing to do. Not leave it to you and your sisters. The three of you might not agree on what we would have wanted."

She was supposed to have said that she would carry on her parents' lives, marry Pete, and keep the farm in the family. If not on the spot then soon afterward. She did neither, despite her father's urging Pete to "strike while the iron is hot." If she noticed them at all, she found Pete's timid attentions out of place at a time when she was saddened by the prospect of her parents' deaths.

With the elasticity of youth, Janet recovered from the scare he had given her, and she cheered him by pointing out to him how long-lived their family was. So, while encouraging Pete in his slow suit, he plotted to help him with a different tack, a more immediate threat, a further variation upon the theme of "it's later than you think." Confident of winning, he was enjoying this game he and Janet were playing. He was pleased with himself and with her. She was calling his bluff. That baby girl of his, she was his match—almost.

The nearby town could expand in just three directions, for it was bounded on the west by the Hudson River. It was spreading rapidly as commuting distance to New York extended ever northward. The Hudson was tidal, and a tide of workers now flowed with it down to the city in the morning and back up in the evening. The local acreage was becoming too valuable to farm, the inducement to the natives to parcel and sell theirs too tempting to withstand. Dairy herds had been auctioned off, orchards uprooted, pastures paved over. What had been a land of milk and honey (bees were the orchardman's best friends: they pollinated his blossoms) had been converted into shopping plazas and developments. Now it was like a game of Monopoly, houses on every square. In all the area the old Bennett place was the largest tract remaining in agriculture, and the neighbors wanted it kept that way. It had taken on a status somewhat akin to a preserve, a park, a public trust.

To get a permit to subdivide and develop his land, application must be made to the village planning board for a variance in the zoning code. A public hearing would be held. It would be reported in the local paper. There was little doubt that he would get his permit; he could hardly be denied what so many had been granted. But just because so many had, and so few places remained unspoiled, there would be opposition. It would come mostly from the city people, recent transplants, keen on keeping things as they were. This he expected, but he was not prepared for the volume. On the night of the meeting there was such a turnout that the nearest parking place to the village hall he could find was three blocks away. Good! Let Janet see how widespread was the opposition to the move she was forcing him to consider.

He was not obliged to be present at the hearing. He wanted to be, to enjoy the hostility he had stirred up. He entered the hall feeling as unpopular as an out-of-town fighter about to enter the ring with the local champion. In the community where he was the fourth generation of his family he had become an outcast. What none of these people knew was that he had no intention of doing what he was there to get permission to do. On the contrary. Getting the permission was his way of keeping it from happening.

The concerns expressed by the citizens interested were civic-minded, concerns for the common good. They worried about the additional tax burden for schools and teachers and buses on the elderly, the pensioners, the young couples just starting out and having a hard enough time making ends meet. They feared for the safety of children on the busier roads. Those roads would have to be patrolled more, perhaps widened as well, would certainly require more upkeep, and all that too would mean higher taxes for those least able to afford them. The county landfill was already full to overflowing. There was the threat to the purity of the aquifer with so many more septic systems. The added strain on the volunteer fire department, the rescue squad, the already overcrowded county hospital. Tourism would suffer from the reduction in the deer herd, still one of the area's attractions. Hotelkeepers, restaurant owners, sporting-goods stores, filling stations, all would feel the pinch if the trend represented by this application for a variance in the zoning code were allowed to continue unchecked. A line must be drawn somewhere.

One person present took these community concerns and alarms seriously. He. Those who mouthed them were concerned for one thing: their pocketbooks, the devaluation of their properties. He didn't blame them. He took it seriously too. If only they knew that he was their masked champion, fighting their fight! Let them raise every objection—the heavier the burden on Janet's conscience. The courtship of that latter-day John Alden, Pete Jeffers, was being won for him in a town meeting, not by a denial of his future father-in-law's petition to break up the family farm but by the granting of it. A weapon like a plastic pistol: harmless but scary-looking.

Throughout the meeting he sat silent. He could not take the floor and say, "I agree with everything you've said. Tell it to that daughter of mine."

However, not all were against him that evening. There were two factions. Those against him, by far the more numerous of the two, were the ones who were there by virtue of other farmers' having done what he was asking permission to, subdivide and develop his land. These were the city people. They *had been* city people and to the natives they always *would be* city people. A stranger could have distinguished one side from the other on sight. The city people dressed country casual, the country folks in their city best for the occasion. The city people had moved to the country to escape the city. Now they were like immigrants who passed anti-immigration laws to keep out more like themselves. These new locals would have erected, running about down the middle of Poughkeepsie, a Berlin Wall if they could.

Those for him were the few remaining holdout farmers. The newcomers wanted to legislate that they go on being farmers and thus preserve for them the charm and tranquillity of the countryside. The farmers didn't give a damn about the charm and tranquillity of the countryside. They wanted to go on being farmers, although it got harder all the time and the reason it did was the steady invasion of these outsiders driving up the cost of everything, but be damned if they were going to be told what they could and could not do with their property by a bunch of Johnny-come-latelies from downstate.

After a period of delay sufficiently long to make it look as if consideration had been given to the opposition before a decision was reached, his application for a zoning variance was approved by the village planning board. Now Janet would come to her senses, marry Pete, and keep the farm in the family. It was not that he disbelieved in the power of love, or the power of the absence of it, it was rather that he could not understand how it could prevail over ten thousand apple trees and three hundred and twenty acres of land that had been her family's for four generations, she the fifth.

"All right," said the real-estate agent, humoring the old fellow. "If you insist we'll list it first as a farm. I can see how for sentimental reasons you might want to try to keep it intact. Been in the family for generations and all that. But it's a good thing you've got that zoning variance up your sleeve because you know as well as I do what's happening to farm acreage in this area."

Seth winced, as he always did, at the expression "farm acreage." It made land seem like something divisible into small parcels.

"And the young people don't want to farm anymore."

"My boy Pete here does."

"Then he's one of a kind."

"You can say that again!"

"Has Pete got the wherewithal to buy you out? Like I say, we'll offer it for a while as a farm. But, believe me, a developer is the only buyer you're going to find—and you'll have no trouble finding one of those. They've all had their eyes on this property for years. Even had aerial photographs taken of it. Prime building land. Highly desirable homesites. Got a view of the Catskills from any plot on the place, once it's cleared. I've had several ask me to approach you with an offer, and they've gone up with each and every one. You can cry all the way to the bank."

It was just what he wanted to hear. Or wanted Janet to hear. Which was why he had invited the agent to stay for supper, unless his wife was expecting him. He was not married.

"And afterwards," the man said, "you can move down to Florida and lie in the sun all day long. No more spraying bugs through the night. No more worries over the weather. You've earned your rest."

"I don't speak Spanish," he said. "Or Yiddish."

Janet refilled their guest's plate. He had a bachelor's appreciation of good home cooking, and he had walked up a hearty appetite today. She had shown him over the property, at her father's request. The place had been surveyed, by link and chain, some 200 years ago. That had always been good enough, until now. Never in all that while had there been a dispute over the lines between the Bennetts and any of their adjoining neighbors. Having Janet pace off the boundaries would bring home to her as nothing else had the threat of losing it. Now the man attacked his second helpings no less enthusiastically than the first. But the elder Bennetts and Pete pushed away their unfinished plates.

Apples. First crop we had a record of. And that pioneer farm family lost heavily on it. They too were forced from their orchard. In apple farming you won a round now and then but you lost as many or more. Why do it then? For the satisfaction of taking on a surefire winner, nothing less than nature herself, the elements. Brought out the grit in you. If they'd had it to do over again Adam and Eve would have done it. Apple farmers were like that. Born, not made. You inherited it. Maybe through a strain from that original couple. And because your forebears had endured its hardships for your sake you owed it to them to endure what they had endured. They expected that of you, no less. What was it that kept us from flying off into outer space? And how was that discovered? Ah, if only an apple would fall on Janet's head, teach her the law of gravity, and tie her down to her native soil!

It mystified him how, his blood fueling her, she could tramp over the property with the real-estate dealer and every prospective buyer he brought out, and not comprehend what a prize she was letting go. By now the agent could have shown the place himself, so many times had they gone together over it, but she insisted on accompanying every party. Offers were made but on the agent's advice, or so he pretended, Seth was accepting none because they kept going up all the time. Yet even this did not increase the worth of her property to Janet. It did to him. It made it all the harder to sell.

"You realize, Pete," he said across the breakfast table one morning during this period, "that with the disappearance of orchards hereabouts, combined with the increase in population, which is to say the market, the price of locally grown apples is sure to soar. Instead of succumbing to offers to sell, now is the time for farmers to hold on. I know it's what I would do if only I were younger, or had somebody to carry on after me. This place is going to be a gold mine, with somebody in charge who knows the business. The day will come when apples are individually wrapped in foil like chocolates. I may not live to see it, but it can't be far off.

"So now, what are we going to be doing today? You're the manager."

"More of the same. Planting trees."

"Planting trees!" said Molly to Janet. "If those two don't take the cake. The place is up for sale, and they're still planting trees."

"This building boom we're in is a bubble that could go bust overnight. Overnight. Then what's left? Farmland. Got you a place with no mortgage to foreclose—and this has never had one since the dawn of Creation—you won't be selling apples on streetcorners. You'll be supplying them."

"Planting trees. At your age."

"We orchardmen take the long view. Eh, Pete? Father to son. Or son-in-law, as the case may be. As long as this remains an orchard it's going to be treated as one. That means replacing trees. Maybe one of my grandchildren will want to farm it."

"You haven't got any grandchildren," said Molly. "And if you were to have one tomorrow it would come of working age about the time these trees you're planting bear their first fruit. You expect to live to see that?"

"I expect to be feeding people long after I'm dead. When you think, Pete, of the work that goes into an orchard! The work and the faith. Your grandfather planted that tree, your father that one. They did it for their children, we do it for ours. Can you just imagine the heartbreak of seeing them all torn up by the roots?"

"I don't have to imagine it. I have seen it done."

"I'm sorry I mentioned it, son. That was thoughtless of me."

An offer was made by a developer which the agent advised him to accept. He did. He accepted it with no intention of living up to the agreement but in order to impress Janet with his determination, with the worth of her patrimony and her duty to preserve it. For the announcement of his acceptance the agent was invited to supper. He felt not one twinge of conscience over using and misleading the fellow. He did not like him, nor any of his breed. Merchants of misery, of broken homes, deaths, ruination, old age, spoliation. Besides, he had practically boarded him.

"Looks like I've got no choice but to take it," he sighed.

Never was so much money accepted so ungratefully. It was an awesome sum. It made him realize as never before what he would be sacrificing. The amount shocked him, shamed him, made him feel a bigger culprit, contemptible in the eyes of all the living and of all his ancestors now turning over in their graves out behind the house. He listened with one ear to the offer while listening with the other one for Janet's voice relenting at the eleventh hour.

She was calling his bluff, forcing him to show every card in his hand. He had now played all but the last one: the closing. Meanwhile, nothing had been signed, all was still pending. Backing out of the deal even after a binder had been put down was a common occurrence. He would gladly refund a buyer's binder.

He could no longer rely upon that telepathy he had believed to exist between him and her. She was younger than he realized, childish. Truth was, her mother and her sisters had spoiled her. People used to do the things expected of them out of a sense of obligation, but today's youth—irresponsible, selfish. It was time for a showdown. He would be tactful, fatherly—all that; but he would be firm, and he would have his way.

"Listen here, Janet," he said. "It's time you and I had a talk."

She agreed, for she had something to say to him.

"*You've* got something to say to *me*? What is it?"

"I'm engaged. Engaged to be married. You've got all your daughters off your hands now. Well, aren't you going to congratulate me?"

"Who is he?" he demanded.

"Rod."

"Rod? Rod who?"

"Why, Rodney Evans, of course. What other Rod do we know?"

He did not know any Rodney Evans. Who the hell was Rodney Evans? There could be no Rodney Evans, for none figured in his plans. Then he knew who Rodney Evans was. He had been a part of his plans but this was not the part he was cast for. Rodney Evans was not a person, he was the real-estate agent—him with hair like a meringue—meant to scare her with. Rodney Evans was the serpent he himself had invited into his garden. Pete Jeffers had lived under the same roof with her for nine months and never gotten to first base; this Rodney Evans had begun his successful suit on their initial walk together over the property.

"It was love at first sight," she said.

"Shame on you, Father! Trying to make your daughter marry a man she does not love."

"But you *will* love him. In time. Pete will make you the best of husbands. You know how he lives. Hard-working. Easy-going. Good-natured. Home-loving. Doesn't drink—or only a drop now and then. Doesn't go out to bars. Doesn't go out *anywhere*. Doesn't gamble. Doesn't chase after women. And there's another thing. (This is just between you and me.) There's a lot to be said for being brighter than your husband. You're not just better educated but a lot brighter than Pete, and he knows it. He would look up to you. You can twist him around your little finger. And I know you. You're like me. You like having your own way in everything. Eh? And why not! Well, with him you would."

"Father, you are becoming more shameful by the moment. You're proposing a husband for your daughter on the grounds that he's not too bright. And he's supposed to be a friend of yours!"

"Listen. Marry Pete and I'll leave everything to you. Everything. Your sisters don't need it. Their husbands have got the most secure jobs in the world. People are going to go on dying and trying to get to heaven for the foreseeable future."

"Father! I will not be a party to robbing my sisters of their inheritance."

"You always were my favorite. You know that."

A silence fell. Between father and daughter passed a perception. It was as though he were wooing her for himself.

"I know nothing of the sort. And I don't want to hear it. How can I face my sisters? If I'm your favorite now it's because I'm the one still unmarried."

"Tell me, what have you got against Pete?"

"I've got nothing against Pete. I like him. But I don't love him. He's supposed to be a friend of yours. Would you want your friend to marry a woman who didn't love him? I like Pete too much to wish that on him. What is more, I have no reason to think he loves me."

"He respects you."

"Once and for all, Father, I will never marry a man I do not love. Did you have me only so I could carry on this farm?"

"It's been in our family, yours and mine, for four generations."

"That's long enough. Time for a change."

"That does it! Now you listen to your father, young lady."

"Listen to your daughter, old man. You are forgetting that you are my father."

"Marry Pete, and everything will be yours. Marry this what's-his-name—"

"Rodney. Rodney Evans. And I will soon be Mrs. Rodney Evans."

"—and I will leave everything to be divided between your sisters."

"You're no father, you're . . . You're a breeder. A stockbreeder."

He fell silent, struck by a truth in what she had said. The difference in their outlooks made him feel the difference in their ages, made him feel that indeed he was not the father of his children—or rather, that they were not the children of their father. Yes, he had "bred" them with a career for them in mind, as he had been bred. He had given them life, that was to say, he had passed on to them the life passed on to him. He had housed them, fed them, clothed them, educated them, nursed them. Yet it was not he alone who had done that. He had been a link in the chain. Fruit from trees set out by their grandparents had paid their bills. Did they owe nothing to those who had worked and worried and denied themselves and put aside for their unborn offspring? Were they now free to do just as they pleased, mate to their fancy, outside the strain, without consideration for their forebears? He had expected that their long-lineaged genes would shape and guide them. They thought the world began with themselves. For him the world was ending with himself.

"Father," she said, "you ought to have traveled. Seen

something of the world. Then you wouldn't think that the sun rises and sets over this farm of yours."

"To have one spot of earth that is all the world to him—that is what I call a fortunate man. That it costs him work and worry now and then makes it all the dearer."

"What reward has it brought you?"

"Independence! I have been my own man."

"Independence! You've been a slave. Ten thousand masters you've got. You belong to those trees. They don't even let you sleep."

"What do you think—that life is a picnic?" he said. "Think I would sooner have had it soft? Sit in a bank making loans to people? Sell their houses out from under them? Brokers in heartbreak! I've fed people. And more than that. Not just staple food. Joyful food. What children love to steal. There's satisfaction in that. No, it hasn't always been easy. But man must eat his bread in the sweat of his face."

"Father, remember how that curse came upon us?"

Going once.

Going twice.

He was like an auctioneer egging on two competing bidders.

Except that one, Janet, was not competing.

Going . . .

Going . . .

Gone!

It was the commission he would earn on the sale of the Bennett farm that put Rodney Evans in a position to propose marriage. So, with a sense of the fitness of it which he expected him to share, he informed his future father-in-law. This commission was staying in the family.

The terms of the sale left them with a lifehold on the house and five acres right around it. At once, even before the clearing of it began, his former land, the land of his family, was like a lake surrounding his little island. Just so he felt himself cut off from his neighbors, his former friends. The very trees, now awaiting execution, the trees whose pruning he had overseen as watchfully as a mother the barbering of her brood, reproached him for his treachery—or would have if he had ventured among them.

One morning a week after the closing they were awakened by noises as if war had broken out all around them: bursts of machine-gun fire, the rumble of tanks. Although expected, it still came as a shock, and they clung to each other, frightened by this upheaval in their lives. The temptation was to pull the covers over their heads and stay in bed, but drawn by a contrary curiosity he dressed and went outdoors.

Men with chainsaws were in the trees as pruners had once been, only these were not just trimming out the unwanted suckers, they were lopping off all the limbs. Above one pile hovered a pair of songbirds protesting the destruction of their nest with its eggs. Already half a dozen trees had been topped, leaving a row of stumps three feet tall.

Now the bulldozer was brought on. It lumbered up to a stump, lowering its blade like a buck his antlers to engage a rival. For a minute the contest was a stand-off. The tree resisted, clung to its hold. Then as though in mounting rage the engine growled deeper and deeper as the operator summoned up its lowermost gears. Its treads dug into the ground. The tree yielded, toppled, its roots tore loose and surfaced. One after another the stumps were attacked. Then they and their limbs were pushed into a pile. The holes left looked like bomb craters. The pile was doused with kerosene and set afire. Being green, the wood smoked thickly. Soon the scene was like one of those days when fog from off the river blanketed the valley.

It was not that he had never before seen an apple tree uprooted, even whole sections of the orchard. Space was valuable, spray and fertilizer expensive, and when trees became old and unproductive they had to be culled out. But those were replaced with young stock.

And so, although their working days were over and they might have slept late now, they were up as early as before, awakened by the roar of the bulldozers and the snarl of the chainsaws on all sides of them. It was as though they were surrounded by packs of lions and tigers prowling from dawn to dusk.

Up and down the roads all around he went on his motorcycle, calling on his neighbors. His message to them was, "I tried to sell it as a going farm, keep it together like it's always been. It was advertised that way in the paper for months, and that paper is read the length and breadth of the valley. The real-estate agent shared the listing with other agents in six counties. My family has farmed it for four generations, and I was ready to sell it for a lot less if only it could be kept intact. Not an offer did I get. Not a prospect. I don't know what the world is coming to when nobody wants to farm anymore.

"I never expected it would come to this. I expected my daughters to marry farmers and carry on as always before. Out of three, one at least one would. But those girls of mine all fell far from the tree. How it hurts me to have to say that!

"Put yourself in my place. I planted those trees. I fertilized them. I protected them against their enemies. Whenever the radio warned of an invasion of insects or mold, I was up with them all night like a father with a sick child. Only I had ten thousand children to nurse. To see them being uprooted breaks my old heart."

You can cry all the way to the bank: those who did not say that to his face looked it.

"Believe me, it's not the money," he said. "The money means nothing to me. What's money at my time of life?"

This was the point on which he was most anxious to be believed.

Then their looks said: *What kind of a fool do you take me for?*

He was ruining life for everybody. A housing development next door, hundreds more cars on the roads, snowmobiles, the whine of lawn mowers, barking dogs, the summer-evening air smelling like Burger King was not what Eugene Crockett had in mind in retiring to the country from the city, restoring his antique farmhouse, trimming his woodlots, landscaping his grounds, planting lawns and keeping them like billiard tables. Bob Johnson was saddened by the loss of his old hunting grounds. "What trophies came out of those orchards of yours! Well, that's the way the world is going. It's progress, I suppose. Can't stand in the way of it." Progress: the dirtiest word in his vocabulary! Howard Simms said, "Well, Seth, you won't have to be out on that tractor at all hours of the night anymore." But out on that tractor was where he wanted to be. It was what he was. Or had been.

Ed Smith asked how much it had cost him.

"How much did what cost me?"

"Seth, you and me have lived here all our lives. We both know how things get done. How much did that zoning variance cost you? Under the table."

What the man meant to express was his cynicism, his inborn suspicion and mistrust of his elected representatives. It never occurred to him that he was implicating his neighbor in bribery and corruption.

Tom Watkins was saying, "Well, Seth, I guess you did the only thing you could. It's not for me to judge you," when his wife Lois burst in with, "Well, I will! You've ruined us all, Seth Bennett. Take a nice rural community and turn it into a country slum."

"Slum?" he said, though he said it softly, not aggressively, not indignantly. "The minimum lots are three acres. And buyers must agree to spend no less than a hundred thousand dollars on their homes." He was not excusing himself. For his part he accepted their fullest reprehension. He just wanted to do what he could to lessen the sorrow they felt for themselves.

"Three acres!" she said with the hauteur of a duchess, and with this scorn too he concurred. Not that her plot was much, if at all, bigger than that, but it was, or had been, bounded on all sides by large holdings, including his, and she had been there long enough to feel a common cause for preservation with the owners of the estates neighboring hers.

"Our life savings are invested in this place," she said, comprehending with a sweep of her hand her two-bedroom bungalow and the one-car garage with its long-outgrown basketball hoop over the door. The humbleness of it accused him as no mansion could have done.

"Now?" she said. "Poof! Gone with the wind."

He felt like General Sherman marching through Georgia, or like General Sherman might have felt if confronted by Scarlett on the doorsteps of Tara.

It was while returning home from that encounter that he had his accident. Molly had always said he was going to kill himself on that motorcycle.

He had intended on that afternoon of his accident to make one more stop. This was to have been at the home of people whom he knew well. Thus he knew there had been no death in the family, no divorce, no loss of income. He knew that the "For Sale by Owner" sign in the front yard had been put there by none other than himself. He did not stop, nor even slow down. In fact, he sped up, hoping that he had not been spotted.

He had not been watching the road. He was distracted by an insight into himself. These rounds of his neighbors in which he sought to explain and excuse what he had done and win their forgiveness were not for that purpose at all. Rather the opposite. It was their disapproval he wanted. He would have welcomed being ordered off the property that he had spoiled. He wanted to be blamed so he could blame Janet.

He went off the shoulder of the road at a sharp curve, was thrown from his motorcycle, struck a tree, and broke his left arm, the good one.

Now, impatient rather than satisfied with the job he had done, he put down the razor. He loosened the drawstring of his pajamas, dropped his pants, and squatted on the toilet seat. Accompanying himself, he sang:

"I'll be with you in apple-blossom time.
I'll be with you to change your name to mine.
What a wonderful wedding there will be!
What a wonderful day for you and me!
Church bells will chime.
You will be mine
In apple-blossom time."

He drew from the roll a length of the paper.

With that right hand of his he was clumsy at everything.

II

"Remember, she's your daughter," said Molly.

"She's yours too. I'm not the only one to blame."

She was helping him dress. Although the wedding party would not begin arriving until late morning, he was putting on his good clothes already rather than go through the struggle twice. With that left arm in a cast bent at a right angle, getting him into a shirt required a contortionist's act for them both. She had to button it for him just as at meals she had to slice his meat as for a child. His helplessness and dependency he blamed on Janet. But for her he would not have gone off the road that day. Ten years of motorcycling with a perfect safety record, despite Molly's prediction that he was going to kill himself on that thing one day.

"But thank you for reminding me," he said. "I'll try not to forget. You might have pointed that out to her while there was still time. I tried."

"Your daughter, I said. Not your slave. She has got a life of her own."

"Yes, and who does she owe it to?"

She went down stiffly on her ruined knees to tie his shoelaces.

"You can't stand in the path of true love, Seth," she said.

He snorted. "Love! Hah! She'll see how long that lasts."

She was having the trouble she always had getting up off her knees. Looking down, he saw what appeared to be teardrops falling on the toe of his shoe. The readiness of women to weep over anything, or rather over nothing at all, exasperated him.

"Now what's wrong?" he asked as a matter of form.

"Nothing," she said. Which was not what she meant but was what he thought.

"Never mind," she said. Which meant, "You wouldn't understand if I told you."

He was satisfied to think that was probably right.

Molly had asked the foreman of the land-clearing crew to take the day off, spare them the noise, the smoke, the dust.

"I'm sorry, Mr. Bennett," the man said in reporting this to him. "I wish I could oblige. Like the missus told me, your people have always been married out of the house here, and now this is your last daughter, and all that. But I can't afford to idle these men and these machines. Why, that one bulldozer alone costs a hundred and sixty dollars an hour. And of course I've got no say over the utilities people."

The telephone company was digging trenches for its

wires with a rotocutter, the power and light company was digging holes for its poles with an auger. The screech of the one and the roar of the other could be heard from a mile off. Yet though these preparations went on, the building of houses had stalled with two. The promotional literature for Garden of Eden Estates characterized one as Mediterranean villa, the other as Adirondack lodge. They stood within easy feuding distance of each other. The raw subsoil on which they sat was fertile ground for burdocks and milkweeds, while the foundation plantings of azaleas and rhododendrons looked like faded funeral wreaths. Although his prospective son-in-law had brought a stream of prospective buyers to inspect these model homes, no sites had been sold. They would be of course when the market picked up again, but for now there had been a sudden downturn.

"Bad news from Wall Street. High interest rates. Tight mortgage money. You got out just in time, Dad."

"No apologies," he shouted to the foreman. "I appreciate your position. You know how women are. Sentimental. You've got your job to do. You carry right on. The bride and groom will still be able to hear each other say, 'I do.'"

On his way to the cemetery he passed the beehives.

In blossom-time, plying back and forth daylong laden with nectar, the bees had distilled and stored honey enough for themselves and for him to market, meanwhile incidentally pollinating apple blossoms as uncountable as the stars of the Milky Way. Thousands upon thousands of untiring helpers he had. They were his indispensable partners. In exchange for their services to him he kept their hives clean, protected them against the diseases they were prone to, in lean years wintered them over with sugar syrup. More than partners, they were his friends. He could let them crawl on his bare skin without fear of getting stung.

Once, or rather always before, the hives had teemed like

tenements, abuzz inside and with gossipy gatherings on the stoops. Now they stood empty, deserted. He had advertised them for sale but had found no buyer, another sign of the disappearance of orchardmen—a vanishing species. Their source of livelihood gone, the bees had left in search of another. They would have to adapt themselves to strange nectars, though it was to be doubted that the clearing of the land hereabouts would leave blossoms of any sort for years to come.

In the center of the cemetery stood a lone apple tree. Though he himself had planted it, it was old now, and time had thinned its blossoms as it had his hair. Its branches overhung several closely spaced graves. He had pruned the tree, sprayed it; he had not picked it. Its fruit had been allowed to fall—an annual offering to those who rested below. Golden Delicious they were, and on the ground they were a shower of gold. He called it "the family tree." With him gone, no one would tend it anymore and its fruit would grow cankered and gnarled, for with him the Bennett line came to its end. It seemed to him more than ever fitting that on his and Molly's tomb the surname should have been left off, for they were not passing it on. Beneath stones bearing their married names their daughters would lie dispersed among their husbands' family plots.

With no sons that was bound to happen. Though it was painful, he accepted that. It did not mean that the world, his world, had come to an end. He was old enough to have known varieties of apples that were now extinct. The Rock Pippin, the Repka Malenka, the Buckingham—the list was a long one. They had been hybridized with other kinds and in the marriage their names were changed. But their offspring were still apples. With him not just the name but the life that the name had stood for was dying out.

He had not bred true to type, and his failure made him feel beholden to these, his and his daughters' ancestors. He did not regret having had daughters but he could not help regretting having had the daughters he had. He blamed each for the dereliction of all, particularly Janet, the one given the opportunity to redeem the others and make herself—as she had been until then—the apple of his eye. A sense not of the impermanence of life but of his long lineage, of his deep-delving roots in this consecrated earth, was what he had always felt when straying among these graves. Now he would come here no more until he came forever.

"Speak now, or forevermore hold your peace."

The "Wedding March" had been rendered on the wheezy old parlor organ, pedal power supplied by the undertaker, while the bride descended the stairs on her father's arm. Now facing the preacher, beside the groom, stood his best man, at the bride's side her father, the preacher's father-in-law. Seated on chairs and on the sofa were the wedding party: the bride's mother, her sisters, the parents of the groom, and Pete Jeffers. He had been invited to stay on in the house while looking for a new job. Farther to the north, out of commuting distance, there were still working orchards, and he had made several trips up there. He had found no opening. He was here now as a wedding guest against his will, and it showed in his illness-at-ease.

"But, Seth, it's a family affair," he protested.

"You're family. Or might have been. You had my blessing."

He was determined that Pete be present both as a punishment to him for having been so unenterprising and as the embodiment of his own disappointment. But though he was demanding a favor of Pete, and a painful one at that, he had not ingratiated himself when, after a second tumbler of it, the hundred-proof homemade applejack began to talk. "It's all your fault."

"Seth, you can lead a horse to water—"

"Lead a horse to water! You never even got a halter on her. How many nights did I take Molly out to some boring movie, even a double feature, only to come home and find you in bed fast asleep? Did you ever even get as far as holding hands with her? Ten thousand trees yours for the asking and all you did was drag your feet! Well, many happy returns of the day. I've got to get through it, and you're going to too."

To make himself heard above the din outside the preacher had to raise his voice. A bulldozer was uprooting a tenacious tree with a squeal like an elephant on the rampage.

"Knoweth any person present cause why this man and this woman should not be joined in holy matrimony?

"Speak now, or forevermore hold your peace."

Ranked like the members of a jury, the bygone Bennetts framed on the walls frowned down upon the proceedings. Forced forevermore to hold their peace, they looked to their descendant to speak now for them one and all, for all as one. The living members of the cast seemed breathlessly fearful that he might. The urge to do so was powerful. It was all he could do to restrain himself. He let his moment pass, but he had enjoyed it while it lasted. It pleased him to feel the power he had to scare them, their inability to predict him.

He had been through all this twice before. Now to come was the part he dreaded most. It had been bad enough the two previous times. On this, the third and last, he was not sure but what his tongue would cleave to his palate, unwilling, unable to utter the hateful words. And so, for a time, while all hung upon his silence, it did.

"Who giveth this woman to be married to this man?"

The father of the bride looked around him as though seeking a way out of his strait. He surveyed his kith and kin assembled for this joyous occasion. It brought to mind, like viewing the negative and the positive of a photograph, the family album he had planned for himself. Too numerous to be housed under one roof, his was to have been a compound of kin, a colony with a common aim. No parceling of the property among them. Its bounty would belong to all as one, and in years when the harvest was bad the hardship would be shared equally. The girls would baby-sit for one another and for advice on child-rearing would come next door to their mother. In time the school bus would again stop to take on in the morning and in the afternoon to discharge their most precious crop. Farm-reared, free-ranging, healthy, happy boys and girls, brothers, sisters, and cousins, with no other wish in the world than to follow in their parents' and grandparents' footsteps. Abraham and Sarah he and Molly would be to their big brood. His last years would be his ripest, his harvesttime. He overseeing all: young minds seeking his advice, young arms carrying out his direc tives. More fruit than ever the farm would produce. On Sundays the women working happily in the old kitchen preparing the weekly family feast, he in his place at the head of the table, bestowing his benedictions, dispensing his wisdom, the table talk about the weather, the prospects for the crop, the market for it, the women as interested in the matter as their men. In the lives of his successors, they living theirs as he had lived his, he would live on, a recurrent reincarnation. Garden of Eden indeed!

The work outside came to an abrupt stop. Lunchtime.

"I do," he said in the sudden silence.

"Then I pronounce you . . ."

The grandfather clock struck: twelve funereal knells. It ought to have stopped forever then, its hands folded together upon this moment that put an end to all its many yesterdays.

Corks popped, glasses were filled and toasts raised to the long life and happiness of the newlyweds. He set his down untouched, and there it stayed, going flat, through the rest of the celebrations. The bride sliced and served the cake.

"Dad," Arnold, the unctuous undertaker, said brightly.

He hated to have his sons-in-law call him "Dad," as all did. It was a familiarity, a presumption. They had married his daughters, not him. To add to his annoyance was the fact that "Dad" was what he had tried to get Pete to call him. It was a way of insinuating him into the family. Tried and failed. Pete had refused. Seth wondered why.

"Maybe it was what he called his father," Molly suggested.

"His father's dead."

"That he's dead doesn't mean he's replaceable," she said.

"Dad, now that you're free—"

He hated to be told that he was now free. "Free" meant idle, useless, finished. He longed for the lost servitude in which his life had been spent, for that was his life, and he feared the emptiness of however much future was his.

"—you ought to travel. Get away from here while all this clatter and mess is going on. You can afford to and you have certainly earned it. Or better still, why not buy yourself a nice little condominium somewhere in the Sun Belt and spend your winters down there? Be good for Mom's poor knees. They've got these retirement setups (he hated the word "retirement") with social rooms, entertainment, dining commons, organized group activities, excursions. Never a dull moment."

Shuffleboard. Ping-Pong. Bridge. Bingo. Exercise classes. Arts and crafts. Disneyland. This after life as a man, doing a man's work, feeding people, his own man, independent.

"Dad? Did you hear me?"

"There is nothing wrong with my hearing, thank you." In fact his hearing was impaired from the years of exposure to the piercing noise of the pesticide sprayer. Sometimes it seemed he heard only what he would rather not hear.

"Oh. I just thought that with all the racket outside . . ."

"I heard you."

"Well, just a suggestion. Think it over."

He hated to be told to think something over.

Asked recently by somebody, "Did you hear what happened?" he had snapped, "No, and don't tell me. I hate everything that happens."

If people thought he was churlish, that suited him just fine. He had earned it. Or had had it thrust upon him.

The undertaker retreated with the air of someone who had tried to stroke a pet and been snarled at.

"Don't bury me yet. Hear?" he called. "I'm still alive!" It was saying so that made him wonder.

Presently the happy couple approached him, arm in arm.

"Papa, we've got something to tell you," said Janet.

"Call me 'Father,'" he said. "You're not a little girl anymore." What he was saying was, "You're not *my* little girl anymore."

"Very well, Father. Have it your way."

"Hah! When have I had my way?"

To her husband she said, "Do you want to be the one to tell him or shall I?"

He hated this new wifely deference of hers. She seemed to have just been put on a leash, and to like it. To think that she must ask her husband's permission to tell him something!

Her husband gave her his consent with a nod.

"Well," she said, "we thought you would like to know that we have decided to take the name Evans-Bennett."

Like to know! *Like* to know! The thought of his name attached like a tail to that detested one! Meant as a sop, it was insult added to injury. He considered for a moment not saying what he felt like saying, then said it:

"I suppose there is nothing I can do to stop you."

Her eyes flashed with hurt and anger.

Meanwhile:

"Well, if you won't I will."

Mr. and Mrs. Minister were quarreling. How unbecoming! How inappropriate to the occasion! What an ill-timed show of marital disharmony to set before the newlyweds!

"Please, Trevor. No. Another time. Not now."

"Why not now? What better time? Who knows when we will all be together like this again? When the hen lays, the cock will crow."

Their dispute having been made public, the husband felt obliged to explain it. His side of it, that was.

"Family. Friends of the family," he said. "I have an announcement to make. One which, in her modesty, my dear wife does not want me to make. But I, in my immodesty, must overrule her. For the first time, you understand. My aim is to add joy to this joyful occasion by announcing that we are expecting."

Until now his grandchildren had been fatherless in his imagination. Oh, they would require fathers, as the blossom required the pollen, but they were their mothers' children, fruit of his fruit. They had been faceless. Now in the features of his sons-in-law he saw theirs prefigured. This child would bear no resemblance to him. He would have no share in the shaping of it. It would be a town child and would speak another language. Onto his stock had been grafted varieties alien to it.

Bitterness flooded him as he surveyed the gulf between his feelings and those he was supposed to have on this occasion. A principal in these proceedings—their very source—he was no part of them. He was the father of the bride, an enviable role—for him a bitter disappointment. He had now married off all his three daughters, one of life's major milestones—to him a mockery. He had just learned that he would soon be a grandfather, another joy—for him joyless. He was now retired from his long years of hard labor, and he was burdened by his leisure. He might almost be called wealthy from the sale of the farm, and the money was hateful to him. This wedding was his wake.

Flashbulbs were gaily popping and this made him leaf back through that family album in his mind. Beneath the married faces of his daughters he saw the blossoms on the bough that they had been. He recalled the many times they had been tucked in bed and allowed to fall asleep before Molly and he went out on the tractor and the sprayer and spent the night in the orchard. They would leave the girls purring like kittens, yet while they worked they worried every minute that one of them might wake up sick or frightened and wake the others and they not find their parents there to comfort them, and he remembered one night when Molly dozed off at the wheel and woke up inches short of going over the cliff at the edge of the land, and they had dashed to the house as if they had indeed orphaned the children.

When the applause and the congratulations had died down, Ellen, in something like anguish, said to Janet, "I tried to stop him. You heard me. It would have kept for another time. This is your day."

It took Janet a moment to understand. When she did she gasped. When she recovered her breath she said indignantly, "How could you think that I would resent it? How could you think that I would be so petty? *That's* what I resent! Oh, how *could* you?"

She was fighting back tears.

"My day," she said bitterly. "My day. Come, Rodney. Let's get out of here."

The time had come for him to spring his surprise.

"May I have your attention, please?" he said. "Will you be seated? Thank you."

He put on his eyeglasses and took from its folder a sheaf

of papers. Then, "As my son-in-law, the Reverend, said earlier in making his announcement of an addition to the family, 'Who knows when we will all be together like this again?'"

It would not be anytime soon. A solitude had already settled upon the house. Once Pete was gone, as he would be shortly, Molly and he would be alone. The girls, feeling themselves and their husbands unwelcome and out of place, would seldom visit. Their old home was theirs no longer. It was not his either. He was in it only on tenure. It was not even his to bequeath.

"The last will and testament of Seth Bennett," he read aloud.

He paused for effect.

His eyeglasses were for reading. He had worn them for years. Thus this was not the first time that, when he looked up from the page, his sight swam. But with those words of his still echoing, it was the first time that this vagueness of vision made it seem as though the world was receding from him, or he from it. He had meant to stun his audience, and so he had, but the one most stunned was himself. It was his obituary he was reading.

"I, Seth Bennett, residing in the town of New Utrecht, Columbia County, State of New York, do hereby make, publish and declare this my last will and testament, hereby revoking all testamentary instruments heretofore made by me.

"I direct that all my just debts and funeral expenses be paid as soon after my decease as may be practicable. I further direct that all estate, transfer, and inheritance taxes, addressed with respect to my estate herein disposed of . . ."

Ordinarily so remote-sounding, pertaining to somebody else, the legalese took on a nearness felt by all, himself most of all.

"I give, devise and bequeath all my property, both real and personal—"

That was the standard form. He would leave no real property.

"—which I may own at the time of my death, wheresoever situate, to my beloved wife, Molly Bennett."

He laid the paper aside and held up the three envelopes.

To all he said, "These contain three checks, one for each of my daughters." To them he said, "Will you please come and take them."

They hesitated. None wanted to be the first to show an eagerness to claim hers, just as, after having done so and resumed their seats, none wanted to be the first to open hers and exhibit a greedy curiosity.

He might have said, "Well. Open them," and with that paternal command have relieved them of responsibility. But he was enjoying their discomfort. He was teasing them, tormenting them. He was corrupting them, and the one whose heart their corruption was breaking was himself.

"All together they represent the entire proceeds from the sale of the farm," he said. "I want no part of it. You will find that they are all equal when you compare them."

"Oh, Father!" the elder two exclaimed in tones of injured innocence, shock. Janet said nothing, but resentment was all over her face.

It was Doris who yielded first to the urge to look. The amount of the check made her gasp. She showed it to her husband for him to see their newfound wealth. Freed from restraint by her sister's example, Ellen opened hers.

"Oh! Father!" said both.

"You'd have gotten it sooner or later. Better sooner. I don't want to have to feel that you're just waiting for me to die." Having settled their inheritance upon them, he could die whenever it suited him as far as they were concerned, or live as long as he might.

They hung their heads in sorrow and in shame for him at having such unnatural feelings attributed to them.

Janet's envelope remained unopened. She now rose, tore it in half and let the pieces fall to the floor.

Her final act before leaving home was to kiss him goodbye. It was a kiss on the cheek but it pierced his heart, as it was meant to do, an icy kiss, not a token of love but the discharge of her last duty as his daughter.

The land-clearing crew had quit work for the day. Inside and outside all was quiet. The ever-burning fires of the trees smoldered on and even in the house the air smelled of their smoke. The sun had set and the light was beginning to wane. He sat alone in the dusky parlor amid the leavings of the party, dirty plates, empty glasses. Molly was off somewhere, no doubt shedding her mother's tears of joy over the marriage of her baby daughter and of sorrow over her leaving home. He toyed with the figurine from the wedding cake of the bride and groom. In her haste to get away from the home he had made hateful to her Janet had left it behind.

Pete appeared, carrying the suitcase and the dufflebag with which he had arrived a year earlier.

"So soon?" he said.

"The sooner the better. I've got my fortune to make. And that's going to take some doing."

"Setting off so late in the day? Don't you want to wait until morning at least?"

"I can still make two hundred miles before bedtime."

"Where will you go?"

"I'm thinking of Washington. That's still a big apple-producing state. There ought to be a place for me out there. I'll write when I'm settled."

"I know how painful it must be to pull up your roots and transplant yourself. But you're young. You can send down new roots. I'll give you the highest recommendation. How are you fixed for money?"

"Got a pocketful. You've paid me well, and you know

I'm not a big spender. But thanks for asking. You've been good to me, Seth. Like a father."

"I hope you make that fortune. I wish you a long and happy life."

"I've said good-bye to Molly."

"We'll miss you."

"And I will never forget you. No, don't follow me out to the car. We'll say good-bye here."

"Good-bye, son. Bless you."

Alone again in the failing light he considered the prospect before him. At its end, both near and far, stood that tombstone with his name on it and its uncompleted dates. His remaining years had become too many to endure, too few to cling to.

Outside, the eddying smoke dimming the air gave to things an aspect of unreality. He settled himself on the ground and leaned his back against his tombstone. He raised the pistol to his head, closed his eyes, fired—and missed his aim.

That right hand of his was good for nothing. ☙

WILLIAM HUMPHREY was born in Clarksville, Texas, in 1924. He is the author of nine works of fiction including *Home From the Hill, The Ordways,* and *The Collected Stories of William Humphrey.* He now lives in the Hudson Valley in upstate New York.

DAVID MICHAEL KAPLAN

PIANO LESSONS

When I was seven years old, my mother decided I should have piano lessons—why, I don't know. We had an upright piano inherited from an uncle of hers on the side porch, and I think she felt it should be used. My father didn't like the idea at all. I'd never shown any interest in music, he said; it was a waste of time and money. Most of all, he didn't like the idea of the nuns. Except for Mrs. Kresky, who lived thirty miles away in Gibsonville, the nuns at St. Stanislaus were the only piano teachers in the county, let alone Tyler, the little town in western Pennsylvania where we lived. "I don't like him being over there with them," my father said, but my mother was insistent.

"For God's sake," she told him, "what do you think they're going to do? Convert him?"

So on Wednesday afternoons that December, my father waited after school to take me to my piano lesson. As our Packard coughed and spluttered like an old, tired beast, we'd drive across the bridge to the Third Ward, the side of town where St. Stanislaus was. I'd crane my neck and look down at the frozen French River, its ice mottled and dirty. Once I asked my father where it went. "Nowhere," he said, and I thought, *The river is going nowhere.* We'd pass

American Short Fiction, Volume 1, Number 2, Summer 1991

tired houses, their yards littered with broken toys, empty dog houses, rusted iceboxes and washers, cars slowly being stripped to skeletons. Often their lights weren't yet on, and I wondered if anybody really lived in those houses, and did they have children like me who also took piano lessons.

"Mind now," my father told me as he handed me a dollar for the lesson, "if those nuns try and teach you anything besides piano, you let me know."

I didn't know what he meant. I knew nothing about nuns, had never even been close to one until I started taking piano lessons, and his words frightened me.

"You just tell me," he said, "and we'll put an end to that. I don't care what your mother says." Then he'd leave me to go wait somewhere—I never knew where—while I had my lesson.

I'd knock on the priory door and be ushered into the small music room to wait for Sister Benedict. The room had a stale, waxy smell and was always too warm, the radiator hissing like a cornered cat. The drapes were kept closed, and shadows seemed everywhere. Above the piano, its finish worn away to a dull smoky brown, a wooden Christ gazed down on me in agony. Sometimes I'd hear doors softly opening and closing in the hallway, but I never saw any people pass by, nor did I hear voices, or the sound of pianos being played by any other children taking piano lessons. What I did hear was the rustle of Sister Benedict's habit in the hall, and then she'd be there, hands folded, lips thin and unsmiling, smelling like old sweaters and my mother's laundry starch. She'd nod and sit beside me on the piano bench, and uncover the keys. "Let's begin," she'd say.

I always played badly. Meter was a mystery to me. I was either going too fast or too slow, or losing the count altogether. "Do it again," Sister Benedict would murmur, and I would try, but still I couldn't get it right. Sometimes when I played particularly badly, she'd pinch the bridge of her nose between her fingers and rub. "Have you practiced?" she'd ask, and I'd nod, and she'd look at me, and purse her lips. "Again," she'd tell me, tapping her pencil on my music book in an attempt to mark the beat. I blinked with frustration as I struggled to find the proper rhythm. I rarely finished an exercise. "No, no—like this," Sister Benedict would interrupt, and then demonstrate. "Do you understand now?" I nodded, and tried to remember how she'd done it, but already it was slipping from me, it was still a mystery and a secret, and I didn't understand at all.

Afterwards, my father would be waiting for me in the car: after the first lesson, he never went back inside the priory. "Did those nuns try and teach you anything?" he asked. "Besides piano?"

I shook my head.

"You let me know," he said.

And then one afternoon everything changed. Snow was falling thickly when my father dropped me off for my lesson. "I have something for you," Sister Benedict said when she entered the music room, and she was smiling, something she'd never done before. She went to the closet and came back with something I'd never seen, a wooden box with a metal shaft and scale. "I got this for you," she said, putting the metronome on top of the piano. "Maybe it will help." She wound it and pressed a button on the side. The shaft clicked back and forth like an admonishing finger. "Play," she told me. "Try keeping up." I tried, but the metronome only made things worse. Like a shaming, clucking tongue, it seemed to mock me. My fingers stiffened. I stopped playing.

Sister Benedict stopped the metronome. "What's the matter?" she asked.

"I—I can't keep up."

"Let's try it slower," she said, and adjusted the metronome. But still I couldn't find the proper beat, and still the metronome clicked back and forth, chiding me. I felt myself sweating underneath my shirt.

Once more she reset it. "Try again," she urged.

But it was always gaining on me, pushing furiously onward with a pace and a will of its own. My fingers missed more and more notes, the page became a blur, and still the metronome marched on, and with every tick and tock it seemed to say, *You will do this again and again and again, you will never get it right, you will never go home again, you will be in this music room forever.*

My fingers froze. I began to cry.

"What's the matter?" Sister Benedict asked anxiously. "Why are you crying?" I couldn't reply. I sat with my hands rigidly by my side, chest heaving, my face hot with tears.

"Frank—" she said, using my name for the first time. "Please—" Her hand fluttered, as if she would touch me, then fell into her lap. "I don't understand," she said. "Please—stop crying." But I couldn't—I couldn't stop at all.

"Stay here," she murmured. And as much to herself as to me: "I'll get Mother Superior." She left and soon was back with an older nun, who wore a white shawl over her black habit. By then my sobs had quieted to short, choked hiccups.

"He just started bawling," Sister Benedict told her. "He won't stop."

"What's wrong, child?" the other nun gently asked. I shook my head. I couldn't say what was wrong.

"He has trouble," Sister Benedict said. "He gets frustrated easily."

The older nun put her hand on my forehead. "He feels hot," she said. She stroked my hair. "He should go home early today."

"His father should be coming for him shortly," Sister Benedict said.

"Would you like to rest until your father comes?" the older nun asked me. I wiped my cheek and nodded. She took my hand and led me down the hallway to a narrow room with mullioned windows that looked out onto a courtyard lit by a single lamp on a post. Snow was still falling fast and had already covered the bushes, the ground, the benches. I'd stopped crying now, but was still sniffling hard. "You can lie down over there until your father comes," the nun told me, pointing to a settee by the window. I went over and lay down. She softly closed the door.

Except for the ping of the radiator, the room was silent. It seemed I could hear my heart beat, and between beats, could feel my life slipping away, my future already receding from me before it had even come, like the soft slip of a wave on a beach. I had tried, and I had been found wanting.

I heard a high-pitched yell in the courtyard. I rose to my knees on the settee and looked out. Four nuns were standing in the falling snow. I couldn't see their faces clearly because of the thick flakes, the poor illumination, my breath misting the pane. One nun had thrown a snowball at another, who was laughing and pointing her finger accusingly. She bent over and made her own snowball and threw it back at her assailant, who shrieked and dodged. And then they were all making snowballs and tossing them awkwardly at one another, laughing and running about like excited children. One tall nun scooped up a lapful of snow in her skirt. Making a chugging sound, she chased the one who'd started it all, who squealed and tried to escape, only to slip and fall in the snow. Her attacker flipped up her habit, dumping snow on her. Then they were all upon her, furiously shoveling snow with their hands. "No, no," she screamed, and laughed, and they were all laughing, until one by one they collapsed, panting, their black habits powdered white with snow. For one moment, no one and nothing moved in the courtyard except the snow falling from far above and far away, and all of it—courtyard and snow and nuns—looked like a miniature scene in the snow globes I'd seen at the five-and-dime. *If I breathe,* I thought, *they will vanish.*

And then they rose, and brushed themselves off, and quietly walked across the courtyard and into the dark.

I heard voices in the hall, the loudest my father's. The door opened, and there he was. "Let's go," he said, his lips tight. We saw no one as we left.

We got into the car and drove away from St. Stanislaus. The streets were silent except for the crunch of our tires. My father gripped the wheel tightly with both hands. "Goddamn snow," he muttered. A muscle in his jaw twitched.

Everything looked different, I thought. The houses in the Third Ward seemed transformed, the cluttered yards now soft undulating hillocks of snow, the stripped cars fantastic caverns. A gutted deer hanging from a child's swing set seemed magically rimed and glistening and frosted. Lights were on in the houses; people lived there after all.

"What happened?" my father asked. "What did those damn nuns say to you?"

"Nothing," I murmured, as I stared at the houses. Through one window I could see a man brushing his wife's hair with slow, gentle strokes; in another, a young couple danced languidly while a little boy drove a toy car around their legs. I thought, *I have never seen any of this before.* We crossed the bridge. It was too dark to see the river, but I knew it must be there also, and that below its ice it was flowing, away from Tyler, and even though I didn't yet know its destination, still—it was flowing somewhere.

"They must have said *something,*" my father said, looking at me hard. "They told me you were crying."

I didn't reply. The car seemed hot and close, and I rolled down my window a crack. The sliver of cold air felt bracing. I thought of the nuns playing in the snow. And I wondered: Could Sister Benedict have been one of those nuns in the courtyard? And I just hadn't seen, hadn't known? I thought and thought, but couldn't decide.

"Well, that's it," my father said, making a cutting motion with his hand. "No more piano lessons! You're through with that." He slapped the steering wheel. "I'll just have to have it out with your mother."

But I wasn't listening anymore at all. I laid my head against the window, and closed my eyes, and felt the rest of my life come rushing toward me, like the French River flowing back on itself, and I knew with a shiver approaching wonder that all of it would be both more terrible and more wondrous than anything I'd ever been told before.

DAVID MICHAEL KAPLAN's first collection of stories *Comfort* recently became available in paperback. His fiction appears regularly in *The Atlantic,* and has appeared in *Playboy, Redbook, Mirabella,* and a number of literary magazines. His stories have been anthologized in *The Best American Short Stories 1986* and *The O. Henry Prize Stories 1990.* "Piano Lessons" is an excerpt from his first novel *Skating In The Dark* to be published this year.

TAMA JANOWITZ

A MATTER OF LUCK

Philip had been living in New York City for nearly fifteen years when he met Sylvia on a brief trip home to London. He was no more American than he had been before leaving England. Perhaps this was the fault of his personality, which appeared to be firmly fixed in a chronic state—not exactly of depression, but a perpetual placidness. He would not have said he was depressed; he thought of himself as rather cheerful. But there was something beefy and heavy about him. He spoke very little, because he had nothing to say most of the time, and he had never learned to fill the gaps in a conversation with aimless chitchat or questions whose answers didn't interest him.

The decision to marry and settle down must have taken place on some unconscious plateau of his brain. He was forty-one and for many years had led a rather wild existence in Manhattan, going out all night, taking drugs, all in all considering himself something of a bohemian. He had come over on a vacation, staying with a friend who owned an art gallery, and enjoyed it so much that Philip wished there were some way he didn't have to leave. Quite by chance he came into some money of his own (his Canadian grandfather died and to everyone's surprise had not been destitute—there was some resentment that the

American Short Fiction, Volume 1, Number 2, Summer 1991

money was left to Philip), and since he was at loose ends he put part of the money into the friend's gallery.

It was a large space in Soho; the neighborhood real estate went up in value, the friend was forced to default on a loan, and Philip managed to scrape together the needed sum. The gallery, once a knitting factory with high tin ceilings, cast-iron columns, and creaky wooden floors, became his. When he first took over he knew little about art; but here too he was fortunate, because almost by chance he discovered a number of very young artists to represent who were ambitious and energetic; they received good reviews and were always on the social scene. One or two of the most successful eventually left for other galleries, a few faded away, but the Philip Marstowe Gallery was often mentioned in the fashionable magazines, and Philip himself became something of a personality.

He was asked to lunch by a *New York Times* reporter who wrote a profile of him, a glossy magazine sent a journalist to watch him test-drive a sports car, and he was invited to the most prominent dinners and events at the Guggenheim, the Museum of Modern Art, and the Venice Biennale. Things were going so well that he had the confidence to purchase nearly three thousand square feet on the top floor of a building near the gallery, which increased so much in value that ten years later, had he sold it, his investment would have appreciated 100 percent; a short time later he bought a small cottage on Long Island from a friend with a drug problem in desperate need of cash, in an area which suddenly became fashionable and expensive.

For four years he lived with a woman named Mary Westbrook Smits; everyone knew her by the name of Westbrook, although early on Philip had caught a glimpse of her checkbook over her shoulder and discovered her real name. She was quite beautiful; her mother was Chinese, both her parents now lived in Hong Kong, where she had spent some time while growing up. But despite her delicate exoticism there was something very masculine about her: her hair was bluntly chopped, she wore manly little boots and no makeup, although this only emphasized the dusty yellow of her skin and the rosiness of her plumlike lips. She sang in a rock-and-roll band; when this was unsuccessful she tried to be a stand-up comedian; finally she settled on interior decorating and went back to school to finish her undergraduate degree at a college of fashion, art, and design.

At the time they broke up she was thirty-eight years old; her age was beginning to show, Philip thought, or maybe it was the existence that they led. By the standards of the time their life was not so terribly wild: he made a point of going in to the gallery every day, though usually not until after twelve; unless she had a class she would sleep until three or four and stay up all night. Once or twice a week they took cocaine in the apartment, usually with friends, and went out dancing or to a restaurant at midnight. His own drinking started when he woke up, for by then it was lunchtime and he would have a business lunch with an artist or a collector or curator—one or two Scotch-and-sodas, wine with the meal, brief stops in the afternoon where drinks would be offered, chilled champagne in his own office. And at night there were the restaurants, sometimes business dinners attended by as many as fifty, sometimes with just another couple.

The alcohol appeared to have neither a depressive nor elative effect on him; it was even a kind of joke, among their closest friends, that Philip had arranged with bartenders throughout the city to exchange his orders of Scotch or white wine for tinted water, because invariably he drank everyone else under the table.

About England he missed only cricket and bacon; American bacon was fried into crisp strips and there was no meat on it. But there was quite a large group of expatriate English living in New York; most of his friends came from this group, and it seemed to him that life in England was staid and dreary. It was entirely possible to live in Manhattan with all the comforts of being around one's own kind, with none of the disadvantages. The Americans made a fuss over him, anything said by a person with an English accent was listened to seriously and with awe, and since he said so very little no one ever took offense at what he had said. They called him up to confide in him and after ten minutes or half an hour, when he muttered at last that he had to go, felt satisfied at the advice their dear friend Philip had given them, when in fact he had said nothing at all. But that was how Americans worked: they wanted to talk, and have someone they imagined to be listening, and it made no difference what the reality was at all. At least twenty people, men and women, believed that Philip was their best friend; what was crazier was that they believed the reverse was true and that he thought of them as his best friend.

Mary Westbrook grew more and more shrill. "When will you marry me?" she said. "You know I'd like to have a kid. I don't want to be an old mother. I think that's disgusting, when you see these little kids and the parents are like old people . . . Why can't you hire me to redecorate the gallery? It's because you don't have any respect for my work. At least let me decorate the apartment. I'm tired of not sharing in your life. The apartment is yours; the house in Sag Harbor is yours. Everything is yours, yours, yours, and I'm some woman to show off to your friends like a flower or a chair, and I don't want to be known as Philip's girlfriend any longer, surely you can understand that."

For Mary Westbrook, the city was a city of sharks, and many times, she said, she was spoken to only because everyone knew she lived with Philip. The few jobs she obtained redecorating apartments were commissioned only because people hoped to get an insider price on the artists he represented, or because someone hoped to get into her pants. Then, more gently, she would say again, "When will we get married, Philip? I need an answer."

He said nothing. He had no answers. This perhaps was the best thing, for she accepted his silence. Had he said he had no answer, this would have been a signal to continue the argument. A person could not argue by herself. When Mary Westbrook took cocaine she was lively and glittering; when she crashed, hours or days later, she was weepy and suicidal. Neither of her moods or phases was connected with him. When they took cocaine together it seemed to be an act of camaraderie between them, and he did not want to give her the satisfaction of this. He continued to take cocaine, for fun, once or twice a week, but since he did not like what it was doing to Mary he gradually cut down to once a month and then even less frequently.

He left for England for a few weeks, to visit his mother, who was ill (his father had died five years before), and to look into the possibility of buying a space to start a London branch of the gallery.

Wherever he was, Mary Westbrook managed to track him down, sometimes two or three times a day. He dreaded to think of what his phone bill would be when he returned, but the idea of arguing with her about her behavior was more than he could bear. He wished she would simply disappear.

It was not that he did not love Mary Westbrook, he thought. But her presence in his life—she did not seem to be *part* of his life, he realized—made him feel somehow weakened or irritated as if the skin around his eyes was too tight or he was sleeping on a needle. She was always so shrill and anxious, and this despite her delicate Asian appearance and her outer manly shell that to others seemed to be exuding brusque confidence.

He had not noticed just how strangled by her he had

been feeling until his trip home. In many ways returning to England for a month made him understand just how much it *was* home to him, not a home he particularly liked—here the weather was always gray, he was just ordinary, he did not have the attention of gushing and fawning Americans. And when he spoke he felt himself instantly categorized, his background made public by his accent. The stale, crawl-space atmosphere of life in London seemed more claustrophobic than ever. But back in New York was Mary Westbrook Smits.

A few days before he was scheduled to leave, several friends organized a party in his honor. There was a girl, Sylvia, they said, who they very much wanted him to meet. He was able to muster a smile that indicated he had no intention of being set up with anyone. In fact, he could not remember when this had ever happened to him before. Usually he was simply seated next to some attractive woman at a dinner party and it never occurred to him that there was any ulterior motive behind the seating arrangement.

As it turned out, Sylvia too had been prepared for Philip, told of his eligibility and unmarried state. Philip wondered if perhaps the English were growing more American. Throughout the evening he was pointedly left alone in various rooms with her; at one moment the others disappeared from the kitchen, at another he was led to the couch where she was sitting and the friend who was speaking to him abruptly excused himself and went into the other part of the room.

She had frizzy blond hair and a long, whippet face, and though he had been told she was in her early twenties he could not believe she was anything more than eighteen. She resembled a schoolboy, dressed in a baggy gray suit. With her Oxbridge accent and steely, pale eyes, he could not imagine why anyone would think they had something in common. Yet he felt strangely drawn to her. In fact, they looked enough alike to be two brothers, or a brother and a sister, although Philip could never have been the sister. Sylvia was nearly six feet; he was several inches taller and his hair too was frizzy and blond, although a great deal of it had gone prematurely gray. Both wore glasses that slid off their lanky, crested noses. His were from the National Health, chosen by him many years back simply out of indifference and then never to be replaced and much admired in the States, although one earpiece by now was held on by tape. It was these small eccentricities, at once boyish but also artistic, that made him so respected by museum curators and painters alike. Business and boyhood, he presented both sides of the picture like a cubist drawing. And with her flat chest, her slouched shoulders and primly set lips, there was something similar about Sylvia. "I've been painting sets," she said. "Though I plan to go back to school, after I've saved up, and become an architect."

At least she was not rich, which put Philip at ease. "I'm going to be in New York, in a couple of weeks," she said. "I'm taking a little holiday, to stay with friends."

He knew the people she was staying with—an English couple who rented in the summer near his Sag Harbor home—and suggested she give him a call when she was in town. It was all polite and formal, with no innuendo intended. Neither of them had any innuendo at their disposal, unlike Mary Westbrook Smits, who flirted wildly with male and female alike and cracked dirty jokes and smoked cigars after dinner, and had been known to dance on tables with members of the corps de ballet following a benefit fête.

He put Sylvia out of his mind until she called, although afterward he would remember things differently and say he had thought of her a great deal during that time. When he returned to New York, Mary Westbrook, though not her things, had departed. A note on the table said she had gone off with a bisexual composer and was in Paris—though of course the note didn't mention Pieter's bisexuality nor even that he was a composer, only that she had met someone else and would be in touch.

She returned in tears a few days later. Naturally, though she was hysterical and apologetic, it was easy for him to be firm and assist her in moving her things back to her parents' apartment on the Upper West Side of the city. Her parents had always kept a Manhattan apartment, though since Mary was a small child most of their time had been spent in Hong Kong.

The apartment was dark and dreary, but it was large and furnished with overstuffed melon-and-gray Danish furniture, with walls papered in slubby beige silk. The last time the place had been redecorated was in 1969. He thought Mary could not have been luckier, not only to have a furnished place at a low rent all ready to move into (she had been living there before she met Philip and had been put in charge, by her parents, of keeping up with the gas and electric bills, though her dad sent money from abroad to an account to assist with the rest), but also an understanding ex-boyfriend to help her move. Lucky! He wished her only the best.

And why shouldn't he? It was a lucky time for many people to be living in, although Philip would not have said that he himself was lucky—it was simply that he had been smart, and though he had been born in drab circumstances (his father had worked as an accountant in the City, and died when he was only sixty-two from a heart attack following a ridiculous accusation of misappropriating funds, though Philip believed it to be from a lifetime of poor diet and nutrition), he, Philip, had lived a zestful life and become rich because he had been smart enough to ride the waves as they came to him and keep his mouth shut in a country known for loudmouths.

In the world's mysterious schedule of events that Philip believed to be his entitlement, Sylvia called and dropped by to pay him a visit. Mary's things had been removed the day before. He cooked Sylvia dinner. He had made a point, after growing up on his mother's cooking, of learning how to cook, using only the freshest, crispiest vegetables, pale green olive oil, and fish he selected himself (when he had time) from the bins of flopping, wiggling crab and haddock on the streets of nearby Chinatown.

Perhaps they had little to say to one another, but it was a refreshing change after Mary Westbrook. With Mary Westbrook it had always been she talking *at* him, criticizing, analyzing, and devaluating people, which made him uneasy. With Sylvia, who was a cricket fan, he talked about sports, architecture, and remote regions of the planet's surface where one or the other of them had spent time. That their conversation never turned to gossip, that she did not criticize anything, not movies she had seen nor buildings nor other people—his sense of relief was so great he felt something close to elation.

They both drank a great deal of wine and she spent the night. In the morning he suggested that she not return to her friends' apartment for the rest of her vacation but stay with him. At the end of her holiday she managed to extend her stay for another week; after a time it became clear she was not going to go back at all, though nothing was said.

He sent her to his lawyer, who got her a green card for a two-year stay, and he put her to work in his gallery. It was, he felt, like two pieces of a puzzle coming together. He had never been a physically affectionate person, but then neither was she. From time to time, at the movies or a dinner party, they would hold hands, or she would give him a quick embrace, but he never felt her to be hanging on him or clutching in any way.

She found a school where she could study, part time, for

an architecture degree; he paid the tuition, but it was of no consequence—it was just that he had money and she did not. When Mary Westbrook had asked him for the money to go back to school, he paid, but with a sense of being used. This was not the same at all. If he worked late, or wanted to meet friends in the evening without Sylvia, she never minded; she had friends of her own, or was happy to stay home by herself. But he found he needed to go off without her less and less frequently.

At the end of the year, without prompting by her or any outside source, he suggested that they get married. He was now forty-one years old, about to turn forty-two; Sylvia would be twenty-six in the fall. In a tone that was neither joyful nor depressed she said, "All right. When do you want to do it?"

"Maybe next week," he said, in the same voice as she.

"I was thinking," Sylvia said. "Maybe we should have a baby."

"OK," he said. "Let's have one."

They were married in a civil ceremony and returned to London shortly thereafter for a party that her father insisted on giving. The friends who had introduced them were very pleased. Sylvia became pregnant almost immediately on their return; more and more of their time socially was spent with other couples with young babies. He was nervous when she announced so early on in her pregnancy that they were going to have a baby; he was not as certain as she that something wouldn't go wrong—she might have a miscarriage, it had been known to happen—but reports from the gynecologist were positive and for the first time Philip thought that perhaps he had wished for too little and should have asked, all along, for more. He could not say that what he felt for Sylvia was anything like the passion between men and women he had read about in books or seen in the movies, but he realized that in the first place neither of them was that sort of person, and perhaps in the end that was not what he would have wanted.

Both of them had smoked cigarettes, but when she quit after she became pregnant he stopped as well, and managed to cut down on his drinking to a degree. It was then that he remembered his father, whom he thought of only rarely, telling him a similar story about his own experiences from before Philip was born. He had had few conversations with his father, who had been a very quiet man.

One night, simply out of curiosity, he smoked some crack at a friend's house—he had always thought of himself as the kind of person who wanted to try everything in life—and though the high was extremely powerful it was brief, and after he had tried it he had no interest in trying it again. Even the idea of cocaine seemed pointless; he and Sylvia had taken it together occasionally, and now she said she didn't mind if he wanted to do it without her. But he thought he would wait until she was no longer pregnant. A friend of Sylvia's held a baby shower for her and he arrived toward the end to pick her up and to see the presents. He had, early on, introduced Sylvia to Mary Westbrook, who had worked hard at cultivating their friendship; she was now very successful, and had a twenty-two-year-old boyfriend in tow, although none of the other women had brought husbands or boyfriends with them. She gave Sylvia a large, expensive mobile, from which hung miniature skyscrapers, tiny pink and blue chairs, little cottages, and dolls with white, blank faces and smiling lips. Sylvia held it up in front of the others so that Philip could see. He murmured how nice it was, and that they would put it over the baby's bed, but secretly he thought he would tell Sylvia, when they got home, not to unwrap it again. He had thought, at the time when he broke up with Mary, that he wished her only the best; but now he was troubled, though he did not know why.

Philip and Sylvia spent long weekends at Sag Harbor,

reading books, playing tennis and walking along the deserted country roads in the fall. In the last months of her pregnancy Sylvia was very lethargic, but the quieter and more dreamy she became, the happier he felt being around her. It occurred to him one night, gazing at her belly as she peacefully slept, that somewhere in his life he had developed the philosophy that it was the invisible who ruled the earth and because he, Philip, had never disturbed anything, he had always received everything he wanted or needed in this life and that this was what he deserved. But where or why he had developed this idea he could not say.

They decided to have the baby in the States; her mother came over just in time. She was a tall, asthenic woman with the same Roman head as Sylvia and the same gray, glassy eyes that those few who did not care for Philip and Sylvia said resembled insects' eyes. Sylvia's mother was a calm, aloof woman; her arrival had been an unexpected surprise. In many ways she had always seemed almost completely indifferent to Sylvia, but he had liked this about her: other mothers-in-law, he imagined, would be utterly unbearable, giving advice, begging Sylvia to come home. All in all, he thought, the gene pool they were giving this child was a good one; he would not have wanted to create anything different.

Yet in the delivery room he abruptly wished for the baby to be a boy and was worried that, when early on they had had the chance to learn the baby's sex through ultrasound testing, they had chosen not to. Any girl born to him and Sylvia would be far too masculine for her own good, and perhaps it was true, as Mary Westbrook Smits had always said (though he had paid no attention to her at the time), that women did have a harder time of things in this world.

The birth did not go smoothly, and he was sent out to the lobby to wait with Sylvia's mother. Finally the doctor emerged. The baby had a number of birth defects: his lungs were underdeveloped and something was wrong with his heart. He would need more than one operation, and even then there was no telling if any brain damage had been sustained. With modern technology, the doctor said, none of the problems were insurmountable, but he did not want to say that nothing could go wrong.

It seemed impossible to believe. All of their friends had had healthy babies; it was only on some schlocky TV movie-of-the-week or in the *Reader's Digest* (which he had read only on his infrequent visits to his mother, or in the dentist's office) that such things happened to people.

He saw then, sitting in the pea-colored hospital waiting room with Sylvia's mother, smoking innumerable cigarettes, that somewhere along the line he might have wished for one thing too many, and that everything he had acquired, thinking it was what he was entitled to for keeping his mouth shut and never feeling too happy or too sad—might have been, after all, only a matter of luck. ☙

TAMA JANOWITZ was born in San Francisco and now resides in New York City. She has published two novels *American Dad* and *A Cannibal in Manhattan* and a collection of short fiction *Slaves of New York*. The film version of *Slaves of New York*, for which she wrote the screenplay, was released in 1989. Her writing has appeared in *The New Yorker, Interview, Spin, Paris Review,* and others. She is working on a new novel.

LEWIS NORDAN

A POOL OF FISH

When it was over, my mother said that she thought the funeral reception had been a great success. "The bluefish was especially nice," she said. In fact the funeral was a nightmare. We never should have gone. It was self-destructive on my mother's part to drag us there. She was morbidly curious to meet Harris's ex-wife Molly. It was Molly's mother who had died.

Our first look at Molly was inside the church. In the pew, beneath the steep beamed ceiling, in the dim light that came through the colored windows, Molly was slender and blond and stricken-looking. We eased into the long pew and sat beside her, Harris and then my mother and then me. Molly's dress was gray silk and she wore a single strand of pearls.

Molly was not only beautiful, but also strong. When others wept Molly comforted them. She was generous with her loss. She patted my mother's arm and said, "Thank you for coming, Christine. It's easy to see why Harris loves you." Her voice was Southern and sincere.

My mother was stricken, too, but not with grief, only with the magnitude of her mistake in coming here. She looked like a person who has started to age rapidly. Jealousy added ten pounds to her frame. Her skin sagged and

American Short Fiction, Volume 1, Number 2, Summer 1991

all its flaws became apparent. There was makeup visible in every pore. The veins in her hands stood up and turned blue. Her clothing looked like old-woman clothing.

I ached for my mother and wanted to deliver her, but I could not. I hated Harris for allowing her to talk him into coming here. "You loved that old woman," my mother had said, and Harris had said, "Well, that's true, I did love her. We were very close at one time." I won't pretend to understand my mother's need to punish herself in this way, I can only resent Harris for permitting her to succeed.

Do I need to say that at age twelve I too was stricken? Not with grief but with love for my mother's rival. After the service was finished and the mourners left the church, I walked close to Molly and deliberately allowed my hand to brush against hers. She looked at me with a tragic smile that made me want to see what women are hiding beneath their clothes. I said, "I'm sorry your mama died."

Molly said, "My precious darling." She took my face in both her hands and kissed me on the lips. The flesh of our lips clung and then released. Her breath was like cinnamon. A part of innocence kicked up its heels and then keeled over dead.

My mother saw it all. She looked at me as if my face were on a milk carton. It was the most joyful, most morbid moment of my life.

There were many people at the funeral. Outside the church, beneath three-hundred-year-old oak trees, people shook hands with Harris and hugged him, and said they had missed him these seven years. Some said they loved him. They recalled how close Harris and the dead woman had once been. Harris agreed. Once I heard him say, "I put off leaving Molly for fear of losing Mom's friendship." A large-breasted woman with her bra strap showing said, "It's just so good to see you and Molly together again." Then to my mother she said, "Oh, that's probably the wrong thing to say, but you can see for yourself . . ." The sentence needed no ending. Harris had worn a gray linen suit, and he and Molly looked like beautiful twins. My mother might have been painted onto the scene as an afterthought.

Molly's beauty found new ways to break my heart and my mother's spirit. Molly did not perspire. No matter how hot the sun beat down, her dress stayed crisp and her hair stayed soft. There was no sweat, not even on her upper lip, where it would have been beautiful in any case.

My mother was not so lucky. She was sweating bullets. Large leaden pellets of heavy-density salt water, all over her face. Her hair was damp and formless. The talcum powder that she had applied after her shower was now caked to her neck. The back of her dress was showing large damp spots between the shoulder blades. She kept her arms at her sides to hide the big wet stains forming like moons at her armpits. She blinked her eyes as sweat poured off her forehead.

She said to Molly, "It was so chilly at the hotel this morning . . ." This was her apology for being unbeautiful, as if she were sweating because she was overdressed.

Molly said, helpfully, "Air conditioning can be deceptive."

Mother said, "The heat never used to faze me."

Later Mother saw Harris steal a glance at Molly. She said, a little fiercely, "Is she still so very interesting to you?"

For a while people milled around outside the church. Molly was attentive to everyone. In a free moment she initiated "girl talk" with my mother—this was Molly's phrase. She smiled about needing reading glasses and about the blisters on her heels from new shoes.

My mother was tongue-tied and miserable. She stumbled over every word. The more attentive Molly became, the greater my mother's failures in beauty and wit seemed to be.

Molly courted me, and I made myself her willing victim. In a hundred ways she told me I was attractive. She brushed the hair from my eyes, but not as you would a child's. She leaned forward to speak confidentially to me. We walked along a walkway, which was a part of the church grounds, lined with flowers. Like lovers, I thought. She asked my opinion on subjects I had never given a moment's thought to, and I found that I had strong opinions on each subject.

I said to my mother, "I like Molly."

Watching my mother reel from this emotional punch, I discovered that there is something bracing and fine about another person's pain.

When it came time to leave the church, Molly found her keys and opened the door to her car. The car had been closed up, so hot air poured out and sent Molly back a step.

My mother was getting no breaks today. She said, "Whew! You could *suffocate* in that car!"

She forgot that Molly's mother had asphyxiated herself in a car.

Harris happened to be standing directly beside Molly, so she turned into his arms and he held her there for a few seconds. There was nothing else he could do.

Mother said, "Oh, Molly, I could just *kill* myself . . ."

This is the way things were going for my sweaty mother.

Molly made things right. She stepped back from Harris and said to my mother, "Don't you apologize for one second, dear. This is something my mother did to all of us. You certainly haven't done anything wrong."

There was something in the word "dear" that was not quite right, but everyone was too grateful to notice. Molly had made the world perfect again.

I thought of Molly's mother in the comfort of her death, in the enclosure of her car. What dreams she must have dreamed! I thought. What dreams!

Molly's home was a comfortable wood-shingled red

barn of a house. Hardwood trees in the front, fruit trees in the back. Windowboxes overflowing with geraniums at every window and along the porch rail.

My mother looked like a frightened child in the presence of all this domestic perfection. This was Harris's former home.

Harris looked at the basketball hoop over the garage door, at the ground cover alongside the terrace, at the fruit trees in the back. He said, "Do you know how to make an apple pie?"

Mother said, "No, I'll ask Molly for her recipe."

Harris missed the sarcasm. He said, "Would you? Great! You won't believe Molly's apple pie until you taste it."

The rooms were large and high-ceilinged. The rugs were Persian and Chinese, decorated with bright peacocks. Harris greeted each detail of his past life like an old friend. He ran his hand over the design in the brass woodbox. He picked up small things from a table—a letter opener, a cup and saucer, a figurine of a cat—and replaced them carefully. On one wall were two Dufys in gold frames, watercolors, a train station and an orchestra. He touched the glass with his fingers. My mother could only say, "What a lovely home you have, Molly."

At this moment Molly's magic began to work.

Molly said, "This is your home too, Christine. You can be such a help to me by believing that."

Life as my mother had known it began to change.

Molly took my mother upstairs. "To freshen up a bit," Molly said. I tagged along behind in fascination. On a large bed with a wedding ring quilt, Molly laid out several outfits of fresh clothes for my mother to choose from. She showed her the spotless bathroom, and she laid out fat towels. She offered makeup—"I've never been able to use this color, and with your eyes and skin it will be lovely." Molly showed my mother her underwear drawer. "Most of it still has the tags on it," she said. Together they chose a perfect outfit for my mother and sent me out of the room. When the bedroom door opened again, my mother was beautiful.

Now Mother did not sweat. She was not haggard. Her skin was taut, her eyes were bright, her hands were the hands of a girl. There were suddenly two equally beautiful women in this house, one golden and one dark.

The true miracle, though, was that when my mother came through that door she was wearing not only her rival's underpants and bra and deodorant, she was wearing her grief as well. Somehow Molly had convinced my mother that she too had lost a parent to suicide. My mother was grief-stricken, and so a hundred times more beautiful than ever.

People who had never seen my mother before now knew her and greeted her and even consoled her in her loss. She took a proprietary air toward the furnishings. She picked up a glass from a table and set it on a coaster. When someone asked where he might find an ice bucket, my mother without hesitation said, "Try the dry sink. Right side or left side, I'm not sure." Like magic the ice buckets were where she predicted. She knew where to find the coffee pot. To someone else she said, "Jiggle the door handle, it sticks," as they went into the powder room. She passed a tray of smoked salmon and bluefish. "The bluefish is always nice," she said to an old lady with big teeth and (for some reason) a nylon stocking tied around her ankle. The old lady said, "Where do you get them?" and my mother said, "We have them flown in from New Orleans." Thirty minutes earlier my mother had not known a bluefish from a mackerel, and she had never set foot in New Orleans.

With my mother under this spell Harris was free to ease through the familiar details of his former home, and Molly strolled pleasantly alongside him as a companion. Molly hooked her arm in the crook of Harris's arm, and they chatted with old friends. Harris said to Molly, "I could clean those ashes out of the fireplace. It wouldn't take five minutes." Molly said, "No, no, thanks, darling, I'll use the old ashes to bank the first fire next year." My mother was directing casseroles to the microwave and accepting condolences from the Episcopal minister. The minister! Even he had forgotten who the dead woman belonged to.

It was an accident that I saw Molly and Harris kissing. The house was large and old and had many turns and corners. The two of them had stepped into a small pantry-like area near the stairway, just as I came out of an adjoining room. No one but me saw the kiss, and neither Harris nor Molly knew that I saw. I stepped back into the room and waited a minute, and when I came out again, they were gone.

I took off my clip-on tie and threw it into the fireplace and undid the top button of my shirt. I took off my jacket and stuffed it under the sofa.

I pushed through the crowd of guests, who were picking at the flesh of little smoked trout with their heads still on.

I went out the kitchen door and down a set of stairs. I didn't know where the stairs led, and I didn't care.

At the bottom of the stairs was a closed door. I opened it and went in. It was the dead woman's room, Molly's mother. It smelled of Listerine and face powder and mildew. No one had been in here since she died, you could tell.

For a while I did nothing. I only stood and looked. The house was built on a hill, so there were ground-level windows. There was a stone patio out one window with a redbud tree for shade. These were the things the dead woman had once looked at. There was a deep pool of golden carp. I could see the dark water and sudden traces of the strange fish.

The bed was unmade, a jumble of covers. For one moment I thought the dead woman was in the bed, and so I took a step back. On a table were her crookneck lamp, her portable steam iron, some postage stamps. Who might she have written to, to save her life? Who could I talk to, to save mine? There was a set of false teeth, an upper plate. There were old magazines, a coffee mug with deep stains on the inside. In a corner of the room were a sink and a mirror and a medicine cabinet. There was a closet of old-lady clothes on hangers, and a basket of dirty laundry. There was a box of sweet powder with a rabbit-tail powder puff.

I lay down in a heap on the floor. I wallowed on the rug. I made grunting sounds.

I knew the isolation the dead woman had felt, for whatever reasons, before she breathed the poison. I cried out, "Mommy!" No one could hear me. I didn't want anyone to hear me. I wondered whether the dead woman had called out for her mother at the last moment. "Mommy!" I cried again, and again I did not want to be heard. I held the dead woman's dirty laundry to my face. I smelled the last odor of her living body. It was personal as a kiss. I found the dental plate and put it in my mouth. I tasted the plastic and wire and enamel and dried spit. I tore my hair and hit myself in the face with my fists. I cried, "Mommy!" I could not keep from calling her name.

And then it stopped. It was over.

I was exhausted. I sat on the edge of the dead woman's bed. There was grit in my mouth from the rug.

I walked to the dead woman's sink and turned on the water. I used a cracked sliver of her soap to wash my face. I used a towel from the hamper to dry myself. I brushed my hair with her brush and saw strands of my hair mixed with hers. I brushed my teeth with her toothbrush.

I sat on the edge of the bed again and took off my shoes. And then I took off all my clothes. I crawled beneath the jumble of covers, which seemed familiar to me. I slept and dreamed of a farm in the Amish country; I dreamed of rivers and bridges and coal barges and of a circus train in autumn. I was dreaming a life that was not my own.

There were voices near me. Naked, I stirred beneath the covers. I was awake now. The voices were Molly and Harris, standing together on the stone patio outside the window.

I walked to the window and watched them. They were kissing, of course. There was only a numbness to feel. They could not see me, though I was standing only a few feet away.

I dressed and went upstairs and found my mother alone in a small sitting room. She was crying and did not know why. She said, "It's as if my own father died."

I said, "It's worse."

She collected herself. She blew her nose. She said, "Well, anyway, the bluefish was nice."

Later we walked outside together and stood beside the fish pool. Molly and Harris were gone, who knows where. My mother and I stood on the broad flagstones. We watched the golden carp in the mineral-scented water. ❧

LEWIS NORDAN is the author of two collections of short fiction *Welcome to the Arrow-Catcher Fair* and *The All-Girl Football Team*. Mr. Nordan's third collection *Music of the Swamp* will be published in the fall. His short fiction has been published in *Harper's, Redbook,* and *Playgirl*. He is a member of the English faculty at the University of Pittsburgh.

THREE-DOLLAR DOGS

All their doors stood open on that upstairs hallway, so the nurses could hear if someone called out. Those old people had buzzers, buttons they could push, but mostly they forgot and just shouted in their thin voices. You could hear everything. It was an elegant house that had been turned into a home for the aged, and it echoed.

Parade rest.

My grandfather would whisper commands and tell me that he was with Teddy Roosevelt in Cuba. He would play a little wheezing make-believe bugle on his fist, blowing *charge* the way Teddy would have liked it. This was his joke.

Al had never been in the military; he was really talking about my grandmother. But Al had seen Teddy Roosevelt give a speech in Butte when he was a young man working the mines. Not that Al ever worked below-ground. What he did was apprentice to a blacksmith, sharpening steel as he put it—picks and shovels and bars—after he ran away from Wisconsin at the age of fifteen.

"Right, left . . . about face." He would be whispering, his lips moving, until he remembered and caught me watching and shook his head. In the silence I could hear the

American Short Fiction, Volume 1, Number 2, Summer 1991

soft footsteps of the nurses on the parquet hardwood floors left over from the days when the house was home to lumber barons, those floors beautiful and polished every day.

"The King of France don't live any better," he would say, talking about his life in that room with its high lavender ceiling and cupids circling the overhead light fixture. The windows overlooked summery afternoons in rundown formal gardens. Beyond the stonework back wall of the garden there was a long hayfield slope to the Willamette River where the water sometimes ran purple from the dumpings of the beet cannery upstream. The foothills of the Cascade Mountains rose into the early mists, steep and wooded like the foothills you see in oriental woodcuts of a place like heaven.

We would get a wheelchair from one of the orderlies, and I would push him along the hard-packed gravel paths between the untrimmed topiary shrubs (dogs and pigs and horses) and the swelling red and lavender and golden beds of summer flowers. We would head down the driveway and out on the street that looped over to the river. Al liked that, me and him and the wheelchair out there on the street mixing with the traffic.

"We're just fine here," he would say, "fancy as the King of France." He'd look to me then, and shake his head, a quick and almost furtive movement, like there was a loose bone in his ear which had been there all his life, and he couldn't live unless he heard its tiny rattle every so often. Just that sharp, habitual jerk of the head. Sometimes he would pass one of his broken hands over his eyes at the same time, fingers thick and the calluses softened but still traced with cracks from a lifetime of blacksmithing, a tentative gesture, as if he might be wiping away cobwebs.

The King of France. Or England. Or Russia. I was frightened and embarrassed by the fact that he would be dying soon, because I hadn't seen him much in recent years. Not that I saw him so much that summer when my own life had gone kited like a bad check. I would sit there with him and worry about myself and money, wanting a drink, seeing the dark bar top, the sweating glass, and my cigarettes and a few dollars in change all neatly displayed like a table setting with the back-bar and the mirror beyond, where I could study myself any time I wanted.

Al was dying and I was too absorbed in such escape routes of my own to ever ask why he would shake his head like that, every once in a while. I would see him, and if I was sober I would be reconfirmed into my own fear for myself, so I brought him candy (which he wouldn't eat) as some kind of excuse for the fact that I had nothing to say, and we would sit a while in silence until he would look at me and grin in his old way and whisper "Son of a bitch" like there was some joke, and I would grin like I got it. That's what this is, trying to get it.

For all the years I was a child my grandfather was a man who got up early and cooked his own hot cereal, and then was gone to build the fires in the California/Oregon Power Company blacksmith shop by six in the morning. Some of that, I'm sure, had to do with escape from my grandmother, who had become a woman driven to planning everyone's afflictions, and with his need for some quiet and isolation before his long day of hammering at hot metal. He wanted his coffee and a fire and a newspaper in the early hours of breaking daylight.

Running away and the men he worked with had become habits too soon in his life, that was what my grandmother said, and I think she was glad to see him out of the house, and glad to see him home when he came off shift in the early afternoon, ready to work a couple of hours unmolested in his immaculate garden. So I'm sure she understood that part of our trip to the ocean was just his need to get out of the house. Maybe he wanted me simply for company, or maybe she insisted he take me, hoping he wouldn't do whatever terrible things she imagined if a child was along. No drinking and no desperate acts. Not that I ever saw him drink, but there were the old stories, like how he was drunk at their wedding, and kissed his mother instead of the bride.

It was early summer and foggy all day on the seashore, hot in the inland valleys around Ashland and Medford and misty gray from the ridge of the Coast Range onward. We were in his new Chevrolet, bought the spring of 1939, as we drove down those twisting rivercourses, and I recall white dairy barns and black-and-white holstein cows on the meadows along the tidal flats and gray, long pilings along the sod banks of the river and great moored rafts of saw logs waiting for their trip to the mills near rivermouth, where the rough lumber could be loaded onto ships and carried off to the homebuilding trades in southern California.

For reasons that now seem extravagantly romantic and runaway, I went back to that coast the winter after he died and lived in a moss-roofed cabin on the outskirts of Gold Beach, reading the journals of western trappers and surveyors with my feet up on the wood stove; sipping at each bottle of Wild Turkey like it would be the last, until I ran out of money and tolerance for alcohol; trying isolation as a cure for numskull ailments of the brain I could not stare down. But it wasn't the seclusion that did me any good; it was the going broke and hiring a cedar log hauled in beside the cabin on credit, and six hard sober weeks of splitting shakes, sweating, and sleeping and getting up to go back at the work until one day I could see some definition to my face as it emerged from the bloat. After three weeks I shaved, and there I was again. I had gone there to live at some romantic jumping-off edge of the continent, and I had learned the simpleminded news that free-fall is no fun after a while.

"So there she is," my grandfather said.

In the oncoming evening we were parked on a headland with low, rough surf breaking in on the rocks below, the sun descending into fog on the horizon. For a couple of days we just drove up and down through the little towns, staying in one shoreline motel or another, like he was confused about what he might be looking for now that he had stood on a cold beach with the foaming water slipping in and out around his bare feet. One blowing afternoon we walked out amid the enormous dunes south of Florence and I climbed them and rolled down with sand in all my clothing while he watched my childhood like it was a puzzle. Then the third day we were north of Florence where the sea cliffs fall hundreds of feet to the breakers and we stopped at the famous Sea Lion Caves.

Since then I have stopped there with children of my own. There are elevators now, which drop a little over a thousand feet to the caves. But in those days paths edged with damp red and yellow flowers led us most of the way down, the succulent groundcover edging to overhang above us as we worked our slow way switchback to switchback, the ocean booming below. We rested at the last crumbling wall of cliffs, where the cormorants roosted and circled their white-dripping perches, and the swirling haze broke open into quick and brilliant sunlight, and we stood blinking and rubbing our eyes like people who have always lived in caverns. The waves looked to shatter in glassy rainbows as they rolled over great offshore rocks. The sea lions, maybe a dozen in all, played effortlessly through the waves, which lifted them and launched them onto the rocks, leaving them to climb to their perches. I hung on the railing with my grandfather clutching at the back of my coat, watching those great animals sport in water which swept them toward the rocks and breaking spray and then receded and came back again until the fog closed over us, and we turned to go on down the staircase inside its box, with windows cut at the landings.

After turning and turning in that squared spiral, we came out into the cave where flickering lights led us down a dripping passageway, and entered the great cavern with its arched rock ceiling where the sea flowed through and the sea lions lived and fought and barked their indifference to us, living on the rocks and in the tides as if no one were watching. There were maybe a thousand or so, and their din frightened me. Through a narrow slit of tunnel we could see out to the open sea, and I wanted to be there. In some side-angle way it all resembled dreams—my parents hundreds of miles away in the dry sunlight over the high deserts, the enormity of the cavern, and those slug-like beasts moving with such assurance through the cold, swaying water. We can only guess at what frightened the children we used to be. More likely it was nothing so specific as my reasons for remembering all this.

Anyway, I wanted out, so we began the long climb. At the beginning I ran ahead, and it was not until I'd spent maybe ten or fifteen minutes hanging out one of the windows along the endless flights of stairway that I sensed something was wrong. Al came slowly up toward me, gray-faced and drawn into himself by pain, one step, and then one more step, resting, and then a few more.

It was then, for the first time, as he rested, that I saw him shake his head in that quick way, and pass his hand before his eyes as though brushing away cobwebs. I can see it now as a thing he learned to do right there, making his way up out of the Sea Lion Caves. When I had gone down to him, and gestured as though to take his arm and help, he opened his eyes and glared at me with what I took to be an expression of great anger. "Get away," he said, except he said it in German, the only German I ever heard from him, and he seemed like a stranger before he closed his eyes and went slowly down to his knees on the damp plank steps.

"Just a minute," he whispered, and he rested there.

He was carried the rest of the way by men who appeared to have been signaled by some miracle until I realized it was my howling that drew them. They seemed to know what they were doing, as if this were something they had done many times before, and carried him slowly up in a wicker-seated sedan chair, step by slow step and then along the paths while he came back to himself and even smiled at me with what seemed enormous chagrined relief.

At the top he thanked the men, and they refused the money he offered, and we both sipped free cups of hot chocolate some heavy-set woman brought us, two or three cups before my grandfather felt strong enough to get on his feet and make his way out to where the Chevrolet was parked along the cliffside highway. For a moment he stood with his keys in his thick hand, dangling by his side, as if he had forgotten what to do next, then he looked to me. "Ixnay," he said, our old game of pig Latin, and then he unlocked his door.

"Three-dollar dogs," he said. Al was grinning about some joke we shared and whispering along about Butte. "Over there they would hunt somebody like you with three-dollar dogs. They'd get you." I had reminded him of the Sea Lion Caves; it was as close as I ever got to going after any cure he might know for the fact that I was thirty-five years old and we were selling out the ranch and my wife had left with the children, and that I was cry-your-heart-out frightened because my baby days in life were finished forever. The North American Van Lines truck had come and loaded furniture in the driveway. I was running the roads.

"That ought to be something," he said, and he was gazing away to the open window as if it framed a scene in which some cheap savage curs of his imagining were direct on my ass, and it was funny. A couple of weeks later he was dead, a natural dying of so-called natural causes. I never saw him again. By the time I got to his burying, the casket was closed.

It's a quick story: I was shacked up in the Eugene Hotel when he died, with a bright, thin woman who loved poetry, which seemed like grasping at straws to me. She was always quoting Denise Levertov (" . . . it is all a jubilance . . . broken fruitrinds shine in the gutter."), and she made me sad because she wanted things there was nobody to give. There was no fuck like the one she wanted, ever on earth, at least as I understood possibility, and she showed me to myself as a fraud and a failure. So I made my excuses, and drove a hundred and fifty miles east across the Cascades to the desert country and the ranch and the empty house and threw out my sleeping bag on the living room carpet and suffered my way into the hangover that was coming, and then the telephone rang on the empty kitchen counter and I found out people had been looking for me the last three days. They were burying Al the next morning; the burying, for me, was a pretty much meaningless event.

What I imagined was Al blowing *charge* through his fist as the casket was lowered and my mother wept and my grandmother wept; I was the one trying to stifle his laughing there at graveside, whose life was the sadness and joke so everyone thought as they averted their eyes, and I saw Al wheezing with good humor while I told him about shacking up in the Eugene Hotel and my terror of that decent, wounded woman who wanted to try it one more slippery time. The King of France, he would say, if I had ever told him anything so true.

You should go up there, I would have told him, trying to make him laugh some more, but it wouldn't have been funny. He was the man she wanted me to be, nothing fancy, just old enough to know better. ❧

WILLIAM KITTREDGE is the author of *We Are Not in This Together, Owning It All,* and *The Van Gogh Fields.* His memoir *Hole in the Sky* will be published in the fall. He teaches at the University of Montana at Missoula.

LYNN FREED

SELINA COMES TO THE CITY

There was no question of a send-off. A group at the roadside with her, waiting for the bus to come. She had a pass for work. Her child was weaned. And she was sixteen. Time to go to the city.

Selina Nsome. Mission station girl. Daughter of the minister's helper. A Methodist mission. A Methodist God. Oh, God Almighty, who took my sister to his bosom, do not take her child from me. Do not take my child. She sang, sitting on her box of clothes, waiting for the bus to come.

February. The summer sun sucked water from the rivers, from the sea, and held it in a heavy haze over the fields of cane and burnt sienna earth. Selina wore her mother's dress, too small across her breasts, but good for finding work. A mission dress, with long sleeves. And shoes with laces. Stockings. A black straw hat tied under the chin.

My sister is dead, she hummed. My twin, my Emma, my light-skin, bad-luck sister. Oh, Lord Almighty, you have punish me for my sister's light skin. Punish the father of her child. Punish that father for his snake's tongue. Punish him for his snake's voice. Punish him for my legs that

American Short Fiction, Volume 1, Number 2, Summer 1991

opened for him when she was dead. Make his manhood dry up. Let the white man take away his pass.

A car flew by, coating her with red dust. She reached into her pocket and unfolded again the address of her cousin's cousin in the city, stared at the uneven printing, and put it back.

"Selina, my friend!" A woman waved from the other side of the road. She balanced a load of firewood on her head, held it steady with one hand.

Selina waved. "*Ai!*"

Mission girls, barefoot, pious. One dark, one light. One dead. *Ai!* Selina hung her head and wept. For Emma. For herself. For the blame she had to bear from her father for nothing she could do. He knew that God giveth and God taketh away. Why had it been *her* that he had beaten with a stick when there was to be another child? Emma he had forgiven. The clever one. The teacher for his mission school.

And now to turn away from Walter, already walking eleven months from his birth, eleven months from his mother's death, and clever like his mother. And naughty like his mother. Dark-skin and fat like Selina. To love so much her own Abigail, light, the color of milky mabella. A mix-up. *Ai!*

The bus curled down from the foothills, marking its course with a cloud of red dust. Selina watched it approach. Time was nothing. Sadness was nothing. The city was nothing. She picked up her box and stood at the edge of the road. She waved. The bus slowed down and stopped.

"*Chêcha!*" the driver said.

She pushed her box ahead of her up the steps and then climbed on the bus herself. It smelled of sweat and the smoke of homemade cigarettes. Some men at the back shouted comments about her hips. They invited her to sit with them. She pulled her box onto an empty bench and sat beside it, her skin and clothes wet with the wait and the effort. She stared out of the window at the poles flying past, the cane, the kraals and hills and trees she knew. Walter and Abigail. Time was nothing. Sadness was nothing. The city was nothing. Men were nothing.

"You're not afraid of work?"

"I'm not afraid of work, Madam."

"Any references?"

"No references, Madam."

"You've never worked before?"

"No Madam."

They stood at the kitchen door with the smells of rubbish from the bins outside, and the dogs whining to be let out. Selina trusted this white woman. She was small and ugly and she never smiled. But she had a space between her front teeth. That meant truth and faithfulness. She had a baby in her stomach. Her voice was deep and polite like a man's. And the cook had told her that she kept out of the kitchen.

"The job is for a nanny. Have you ever looked after children?"

Selina dropped her eyes to the floor. "Yes Madam."

"Whose?"

"I'm got a baby, Madam. My sister she died, I'm got her baby too."

"Good heavens! How old are these children?"

"Not yet one year, Madam."

"I see." The white woman looked doubtful.

"The children they stay with their grandmother," Selina said quickly. "They stay at the mission station."

The white woman nodded. She looked at Selina for a long time, at her face, her hands, the dress she wore. "Well, Selina," she said at last. "I'll tell you that I like you.

You seem to be a nice sort of girl. Clean. Willing. And honest. I hope I'm not wrong."

"You not wrong, Madam."

"But you're *young*. And there will be *lots* of work. My son is eight years old. My daughter is seven. And the new baby is coming in five months. The Master and I are often gone."

"Yes Madam. I can work." Why two and then one, Selina wondered? She stared at the ground, waiting and hoping.

"When can you start?"

"Today, Madam."

"Well then, fetch your things. I'll tell Agnes, the cook, to have your room prepared.—Oh, and Selina, we're going to have to do something about your body odor."

"Yes Madam." What was the white woman talking about? She would have to ask her cousin's cousin.

"I'll provide you with Mum to start with and then you must buy your own. You must use it *every* day. Agnes will give you soap. And uniforms."

"Thank you Madam."

The cousin's cousin told her she was lucky. A room and a bed to herself. New uniforms. Boys' meat every night. But still it was lonely to sleep in a room all alone. No roosters in the morning. No fire smell. No goats. No mission bell. No singing. "Rock of Ages," she hummed to herself. But her humming couldn't fill up her head. Her sadness stopped her wanting the meat. She gave hers to the others. At night she cried softly into her pillow and made it wet. Where was the lucky? She wanted Walter. She wanted Abigail. She wanted Emma. But Emma was dead.

Only the children made her happy. Even the bad one, the jealous girl. Even when they used bad words and pulled off her cap and hid it away from her. They could make her laugh, like brothers and sisters.

"Selina, you mustn't allow those children to be rude to you."

"They not rude, Madam."

She never gave them away. And the children, in return, did not turn their play into oppression.

On her days off she visited her cousin's cousin. Or her cousin's cousin came to her. When she took the children to the park on Saturday afternoons she met other nannies. They sat in the shade and talked while the children climbed and ran and fought. She stood with the nannies who pushed small children on swings and listened to what they had to say about life in the city.

Selina learned a lot. She learned to knit and to crochet. On Thursday afternoons now she would put on her dress and lace-up shoes and walk down through the race course to town. The other nannies had told her that wools and cottons were cheap in Indian town. And so she went there. They had warned her that Indians cheat. So she shook her head at the prices they asked. Until they stopped following her out of the shop. Then she paid the last price. Her new friends told her how to sell her doilies and tea cosies to Billinghams. And how to buy a postal order so that no one could steal her money when she sent it home. They warned her not to argue with a Madam. To stay silent even in anger. They told her how to make sure she didn't get a baby. But she shook her head at this. "*Hayi!*" she said. And then they laughed. Because she was beautiful. And the houseboys and gardenboys always shouted to her as she passed.

One day she learned how to get a whole weekend off to go home. You must write a letter and tell them to send a telegram back, they said. "Mother sick come home." Then you must take it to the Madam and look sad. She won't believe you but she will let you go. And you must always come back on time, they warned.

Selina wrote the letter.

"Madam," she said, standing at the lounge door, dropping her chin, staring at the floor.

"What is it, Selina?"

"Madam, a telegram—" She held out the envelope.

The Madam rolled her eyes and shook her head. "Don't tell me, I know already. Your aunty is sick and you have to go home. That it?"

"My mother, Madam."

The Madam sighed. It was OK. "*When?*" she demanded.

But Selina just stared at the ground as instructed.

"Well, I suppose I have no choice." She sighed again. "Although you *could* have picked a better moment. Three weeks until this baby arrives. P.G."

"Yes Madam."

"All right, Selina. Leave on Friday after dinner. And be back by Sunday night."

But Selina didn't move.

"What now?"

"Madam, Friday is the first of the month. Many *tsotsis* on the buses." She had knitted clothes for the children, bought biscuits for them and packets of sweets. She had collected money in an envelope. She didn't want her treasures stolen, herself in the hospital with a knife in her ribs.

Another sigh. "Thursday evening then. And Selina, this had better *not* happen too often."

"No Madam. Thank you Madam."

The bus was crowded and hot. Selina stood for the first two hours. But then people got off. She saw her world again through the windows. The river dried up now. Cattle on the high ground, huddled together amongst the wattles.

The bus passed the coolie store and then the dam. "*Ai!*" she called out. "*Lapa.*"

It slowed and squeaked and stopped. Selina climbed out into the dust with her new cardboard suitcase. Someone waved at her from the well. She waved back. As she approached the mission a few of the kraal dogs came out and barked and wagged around her, sniffing the city in her clothes and on her skin.

She could hear singing in the church and from the children playing games with stones. She stopped and put down her suitcase. People had seen her now. Some of them called out. The children ran toward her hoping for sweets. Then she saw her mother come out of the hut wiping her hands on her skirt. She saw Walter, strutting now, behind her. And Abigail on her back. Nothing was different here. Time was nothing. Sadness was nothing. The city was nothing. She was nothing.

The doctor had come already for the Madam. But the Madam didn't scream or even shout. Selina laughed. White women liked to shout at the wrong times.

It was Sunday. She had been sent into the garden with the children to wait, and sat with her knitting under the avocado pear tree. "Nearer, my God, to Thee," she warbled to herself. Maybe another boy. It would be better for the Master. For the jealous one too.

The white nurse was up there for the baby. Do this, do that! Selina spat on the ground. What kind of nurse with no baby of her own? Old too, ugly too. Uglier than the Madam.

Someone shouted. And faintly, under the voices, there was the cry of a baby. Selina's breasts grew hard. Her womb tightened. She stood up to listen. A baby crying, crying. There were tears in her own eyes. Her chest weeping, her womb mourning.

A window flew open. "A girl! Another girl!" But the children were in the tree shouting and didn't hear.

"*Wê* Andrew! *Wê* Margaret! Come down! You got a sister! Your mother she have a girl!"

Despite the Madam's warning, another telegram came for Selina. The baby was walking already, round and round, with Selina at the end of her arm. Selina took the envelope from Agnes.

"You better watch out," Agnes said.

"Come home immediately. Walter dead."

"*Aiii!*" Selina shrieked. She picked up the baby and ran to the kitchen. "*Aiiii!*" Not once did she doubt the truth of the message. Dead. Dead. Dead like his mother. The baby in her arms began to whimper.

"All *right,* Selina. All *right,* my girl. Calm *down!* I *do* believe you. You may go tonight. Right away if you wish." The Master watched her sniffing and snorting. "Come," he said. "I'll drive you to the bus stop."

"Thank you Master."

"Do you need money for the funeral?"

For a cow, yes. Or at least a goat. Some beer. A box to bury him in. "Thank you Master."

"What did he die of? Do you know?"

But she knew enough, even in her grief, not to answer this. TB or cholera, and they wouldn't have her back. "Master, the child he always been sick."

When she returned, the Madam called the white doctor to the house to check her up. He looked everywhere—ears and mouth and front and back. Even between her legs. But he couldn't find her sick. It was a sickness in her heart that she suffered. She didn't sing any more. She sat still, like a rock or a chair, and let the baby climb all over her.

One day, when the Madam and the Master were gone

out, the baby pinched her breast. She jumped. It pinched again and laughed. She laughed. They were in the gazebo. No one could see. She picked up the baby, fat and laughing, held it in her arms like an infant. She kissed the baby's hair, kissed its mouth, held it tight against her. It laughed and laughed, pinched her again. Then she plunged her hand into her uniform and pulled out her round, plump breast. The baby poked at it with small fingers. She picked up the nipple and pushed it to the child's mouth. It looked up at her, not remembering what to do. "*Mê! Mê!*" Selina said, sucking in the air with her lips. "*Mê!*" The baby closed its mouth on her nipple and blew. It laughed at the noise. Then it took the breast in two hands and sucked. Sucked so that Selina's thighs weakened and her womb cried out. She clasped the baby to her and rocked back and forth, back and forth. "*Ai, ai, ai,*" she crooned. "*Ai, ai, ai.*"

That night, when the next-door houseboy came to visit, she didn't chase him away. She opened her legs to him. And again the next night. And again. And again. She didn't remember what the other nannies had told her. She only waited for her work to be over, for the dark of her room and her dark night lover.

A few months later it had happened. No bleeding. The sickness. She went to her friends and asked what to do. They told her about the woman with the needle, and then about the doctor at the hospital who would fix you for good afterward if you liked.

She went one night to the woman with the needle. Paid, suffered, bled. The next week she told the Madam she wanted that doctor to fix her. Her friends told her white women would pay.

"But, Selina," this one said, "are you *certain* about this? Look how you love Elizabeth. Don't you want time to think it over?"

Selina shook her head. "Madam, I can pay you back every month."

"It's not the *money,* Selina! Of *course* I'll give you the money! It's just that I want you to be sure you understand what you're doing."

"I understand, Madam."

So now there was only Abigail. And a box for her future. For her to be a teacher like Emma. Selina's friends told her about a bank. The savings book where they wrote down the money so that no one could steal it away. On Thursday she walked to town with her chocolate box of notes and coins under her arm. She stood in the Non-European line and waited.

"I have to count all *this?*" the white lady said.

"Yes Madam. Please Madam."

The woman counted. But Selina knew already how much it was.

"Madam, *four*teen," she said. "Not thirteen."

"*What?* You don't trust me, you monkey? Here, let's see you count it yourself."

Slowly Selina counted while the white lady sighed and rolled her eyes. Carefully she separated the coins into units, the notes into piles. "*Four*teen, Madam," she said.

"Ugh! Jeeslike!" the woman said. "One pound off and you'd think it's the end of the world!"

One Sunday, before Christmas, Selina's mother brought Abigail on the bus. They needed more money, she said. A window for the house. Bricks.

"What house?" Selina asked.

"For the mission teacher. For Abigail. Your house."

Seventeen and sixpence in the box. Selina spilled it into her mother's lap. Her mother's hand shook as she spread out the change. Getting old, Selina thought.

The old woman took the money and left the child with

Selina. A quiet child, she sat on the floor of Selina's room. If Selina gave her a sponge or a comb or a flower, she stared into it, turned it over, and put it down again. A good child. Never cried. Not when Selina left her alone in the room. Not even when the food was late.

"Madam, my child she's here."

"Yes, I noticed that, Selina."

Selina stared at the floor.

"It's a lovely baby, Selina, but who's looking after it?"

"I look after, Madam."

"What about when you're working?"

"The child she is a good child, Madam."

"How old is she?"

"More than two years, Madam."

"And how long—you know she can't *stay* here, don't you?"

"Yes Madam.—Madam, Christmas—"

"What?"

"Please Madam, give me Christmas. I take the baby back."

"No Selina. I'm *very* sorry. How on *earth* do you think we'll manage on our holiday without a nanny for Elizabeth?"

Selina hung her head. Some white women's questions needed no answers.

"You'll have to take the child back before we go." She sighed. "Next Saturday I suppose. You know, this is beginning to be a nuisance, Selina?"

"Yes Madam. Sorry Madam."

The children met on the laundry lawn when the Madam was sleeping. Face to face they stood and stared at each other like dogs. Selina and Dora watched from the shade of the laundry-room door.

"Play! Play!" Selina whispered.

But Abigail looked down now, well taught to keep her

eyes from the soul of another. The smaller one swaggered around the stranger, wearing only a wet nappy. Dora and Selina laughed softly at the wet nappy, at the monkey face and monkey look of her. Little white monkey, little white monkey. Black child with money locked up in a bank. Quiet black child with the time to learn. They clucked in pleasure like aunties.

Closer and closer the monkey came. She pushed the stranger and nearly fell backward herself with the effort. But the stranger was firm and stout like her mother. She stood still and looked at the grass.

The women in the doorway laughed at the contest. "Oo-hoo! Ee-hee!"

At their laughing the monkey jumped on her wide-apart feet and grabbed at the stranger's arm. She bit down on the plump black hand with her small, sharp teeth.

"*Ai!*" The black child ran, without tears, behind her mother's skirt. Hung on tight.

"Na! Na!" The monkey ran too, held up her arms to be picked up, danced from foot to foot and cried loudly, also without tears. She stared down over Selina's shoulder at the other. Bounced in Selina's arms to ungrasp the stranger from the skirt.

"*Thula!*" Selina whispered. "*ukuThula!*" She patted the monkey's nappy softly. "*Thula! Thula!*"

But behind now, into the skirt, tears came. And small low grunts. Rhythmical, breathy with a year-old cough.

"*Thula!*" Selina scolded over her shoulder.

The grunts only grew into sobs, low and insistent.

Selina reached behind her with one hand and hit, hard, the back of her own child's head.

"Aaaah!" the child wailed, high and low, the sound broken into two notes by the damp in her lungs.

And now the monkey too cried. Real tears. Clung tight around Selina's neck and shrieked.

A window flew open half an hour before the end of sleep

time. "*What* is going on out there? Selina? Dora? *Why* is Elizabeth crying so loudly?"

Selina moved out of the shade to be shouted at properly. But Abigail moved out with her, still clinging to her skirt. And Elizabeth, yoke between two mothers, opened her monkey mouth wide at her mother above and yelled in outrage.

"If this is what is going to happen every time you bring that child here, Selina, I'm going to have to forbid it. Do you understand?"

"Yes Madam. Sorry Madam."

The children wailed high and low.

"Selina, deal with those children please. Give them a biscuit or something."

"Thank you Madam."

The window slammed shut.

"*ukuThula!*" Selina shouted. She turned, Elizabeth still over her shoulder, and slapped Abigail on her fat wet cheek. Pulled her up roughly by the arm and dragged her, her legs just above the ground, back through the compound gate and into her room. Slammed the door shut. "*Thula!*" she shouted. "*Inhlupheko!*"

Nothing looked new. No smoothed-out place for a new house. Selina stopped on the koppie for a better view.

"Gogo! Gogo!" Abigail struggled down off her hip and ran.

The old woman staggered under the impact of the child in her arms. She sat down on a rock and let the child lay her head on her lap.

"Where is the house?" Selina asked.

The old woman giggled, clasped one hand over her mouth. "Over there!" She flung a ragged arm toward the station and the kraal.

"Gogo! Gogo!"

Things smelled funny this time. Goat excrement. Human excrement. Even the smokiness of the thatch. Even her mother—Kaffir beer sweetness mixed now with the sweet smell of her old age.

"There is no house."

The old woman shook her head.

"Mother, where is my seventeen and sixpence?"

"Ha! Ha!"

No house, no bricks, no window. The money gone on beer.

"Mother, what about my child?"

Abigail clung fast to the old woman, closing her eyes against Selina's claim.

"No more money for a house!" Selina planted her hands on her hips.

"No money for food," the old woman croaked. "How will we feed your child?"

"Where is Father? I will give Father my money."

"He will give it to me." She peeled her old lips back from pink gums and cackled.

"Gogo! Laugh for me!"

"Hee-hee! Hee-hee! Your uncles are gone. Your brothers are gone. Your sister is dead. Only me."

An old man came out of the church in threadbare black vestments. He stood for a moment in the sun, shaded his eyes with his hand.

The child ran to him.

He bent to pat her head. "*Ai! Ai!*" he said.

"Father!" Selina shouted.

He turned away from her with the child's hand in his. "The Lord's my shepherd, I'll not want," he sang in a deep, rich baritone.

Selina picked up her suitcase and followed him. "Father! Mother buys drink with my money. What will happen to my child?"

"He makes me down to lie . . ."

Abigail laughed, danced next to him to the rhythm of his singing.

"I work hard for that money. I have a book from the bank. Maybe a Christmas bonsella too."

" . . . In pastures green: He leadeth me the quiet waters by."

Selina stood at the swings now, pushing with the other nannies.

"Higher! Higher!"

They had told her how to send food home through the post. Not money any more. Now they told her to pay the teachers straight. Buy the books herself. Or, better, to ask the Madam. Also for paper, pencils, crayons. Madams liked to be asked for these things.

"Selina! Higher!"

For old uniforms too. Uniforms made children proud to learn. They showed her how to take them in, or to open the seams and put in an extra panel to make them bigger. She was lucky, they said. She worked for rich people. Her Madam gave her old clothes. Other Madams made you pay.

But mine, Selina told them, gives the best things to poor white people. And they all laughed at that. Poor white people! Hee-hee! Hee-hee!

Anyway, she is too small, Selina said. Tiny feet and tiny dresses. She pinched her fingers to the size of a fly. Poor white people must be very, very tiny. They all laughed again.

Selina, you are a city girl now, they told her. You are one of us.

Selina nodded. Yes. She knew. She counted her things. A carpet on the floor. Two mattresses already on the bed. A pink glass vase with florists' bows from the Madam's bouquets. Kotex. Mum. Two pairs of shoes. And now a wireless of her own to plug in anywhere.

The white child is growing, they said. Your Madam is too old for having more babies. You must look for another job.

Hayi! Selina said. No more nanny. Soon Agnes would leave to get married. No more Agnes.

Good riddance to bad rubbish, they said.

I could cook, Selina said. Who cooks on Agnes' day off? Selina! Selina can copy those recipes out of a book just like her. The only problem is twenty minutes and thirty minutes.

We can show you how to do it with the clock, they said.

"Madam—"

"Yes Selina."

"When Agnes she go—"

"Yes Selina?"

"Madam, I can cook."

"*You* want to be cook?" The Madam liked to sound surprised.

"Yes Madam."

"There's a lot to learn."

"I can learn, Madam."

She frowned, pretended to think. "All right, Selina. You've been a faithful and honest nanny. I'd like to give you a chance."

"Thank you Madam."

"I'll tell Agnes to start teaching you tomorrow. Mind you, listen carefully."

"Yes Madam. Thank you Madam."

"Oh, Lord Almighty," Selina hummed as she stirred the soup. "You took my father, I gave you a cow. You took my nephew, dark like me. You took my light-skin, bad-luck sister. Don't take my light-skin child from me. Every day I sing to you and you can hear, I know. I kneel down every night. I read your Bible. Sometimes I do bad things. But I say sorry. I am human, you know that. You have punish me. My time is nothing. My sadness is nothing. I am nothing, I know that. Working, working for my child. And praising the Lord, I sing my song to you. But you know that. You know everything already." ❧

LYNN FREED was born in Durban, South Africa, and came to the United States in 1967. She has published two novels *Heart Change* and *Home Ground* and short stories, essays, and reviews in *Harper's, The New York Times, Mirabella,* and *Zyzzyva*. She has received fellowships from the National Endowment for the Arts and the Guggenheim Foundation. Ms. Freed lives in Sonoma, California, and is completing her third novel.